venus

a love story

ariel n. anderson

VENUS: A LOVE STORY

Cover design & graphic design by Maria Spada

eBook ISBN: 979-8-9882962-7-0
Paperback ISBN: 979-8-9882962-8-7

First Edition: July 2025

10 9 8 7 6 5 4 3 2 1

PROCEED WITH CAUTION

It's an Ariel N. Anderson novel, so don't think you won't hurt a bit before you get to that happily ever after!

Please be aware that ***this book contains a major plot spoiler for Under Your Scars***, another novel by me. While it is not necessary for you to read *Under Your Scars* before this book, I would recommend reading it first if it's on your TBR!

<u>Triggers in this one include:</u>

discussions of infertility, mention of a stillbirth (not the FMC's), mention of a possible miscarriage, major burn injuries, scarring, death, and grief.

Please take care of your mental health.

A small portion of all Ariel N. Anderson titles are donated to the American Foundation for Suicide Prevention.

National Suicide Prevention Lifeline:

1-800-273-8255

"Hehe. They called him cooter."

– My Husband

PLAYLIST

How Far Will We Take It? - Orville Peck & Noah Cyrus

Flatliner - Cole Swindell & Dierks Bentley

Kiss You In the Morning - Michael Ray

Don't You Wanna Stay - Jason Aldean & Kelly Clarkson

She Can - Leaving Austin

Lover - Taylor Swift

When You Say Nothing At All - Alison Krauss & Union Station

Save a Horse (Ride a Cowboy) - Big & Rich

Good Riddance (Time of Your Life) – Green Day

Chapter 1 | Vulcan

"Westwood! Move your ass!"

I grunt, the sound catching in my throat like a dry engine start. I pick up the pace even though I'd rather wrestle a live gator than run before sunrise. I can lift a fire hose and haul a ladder three stories up in full turnout gear, but cardio? Cardio is my mortal enemy.

Actually, my upstairs neighbor is my mortal enemy.

I catch up to my crew in a few long, annoyed strides. We're halfway through our mandatory weekly group run, and I'm already bargaining with God to make shin splints a legitimate medical excuse to quit. I fall in beside Trevor, who's been my ride-or-die since day one of fire academy.

"Jesus," he says, barely out of breath. "Did you stay up late crying over Hallmark movies again?"

"Nope," I reply, "just another riveting night of interpretive dance from the bowling league upstairs."

He laughs. "How many people do you think live up there? From the sound of it, I'm guessing a herd."

"Four. I've counted. I don't know what kind of voodoo keeps them going, but I haven't had uninterrupted sleep in weeks."

Trevor snorts and slows slightly to match my pace. "You should get laid. Or at least punched in the face. Either way, you'd sleep better."

I'm almost thirty, so the *just get laid* solution doesn't hold the same magic it used to. Hookups used to be fun. Now they mostly feel like eating cotton candy for dinner.

Satisfying in the moment, but kind of painful afterward.

"Tell you what," Trevor says, already scheming, "Wednesday night. Cold beers and a room full of long-legged women. What do you say? I'll be your wingman. The ladies love a man in uniform."

"We won't be in uniform, you Muppet."

I roll my eyes and try not to collapse as we come to a stop in front of Station One. Our shoes scrape the pavement, and the crew starts their usual post-run rituals: water-chugging contests, bent-over heaving, and light bickering about who's faking shin pain. I do none of that. I drop flat onto my back in the middle of the parking lot and welcome death with open arms. I hope the devil will make it quick.

"Vulcan," Jackson says, looking down at me. "Your biceps are the size of commercial jetliners. How are you getting beat by a two-lap jog?"

"Shut up," I wheeze, catching the bottle he tosses to me.

"He's saving his cardio for the bedroom," Trevor says, like a proud hype-man.

"Jacking off doesn't count as cardio," Jackson fires back.

"You've clearly never done it right."

They laugh. I shake my head and sip my water, grateful for the bond between us. These men are my brothers. Some have been doing this job since I was in elementary school. Others, like Trevor and Jackson, started with me. We fought fires, earned our shields, and even grew our station mustaches together.

Well...except me.

Blond mustaches just make me look like an unfortunate extra from Super Troopers. So I keep my face clean-shaven, which probably makes me the only firefighter under thirty without facial hair.

We head inside to officially relieve the night shift. The smell of coffee, engine grease, and whatever Jackson cooked last night lingers in the air. An UberEats driver arrives carrying five greasy bags of heaven: breakfast burritos, courtesy of an elderly woman we helped with a false carbon monoxide alarm two weeks ago.

She insists we saved her life. Honestly, I think she just enjoys feeding a bunch of idiots who remind her of her sons.

I claim four burritos and protect them with my arms like a dragon hoarding gold. Trevor and Jackson mock me with dramatic gasps.

"Are you eating for three?" Jackson asks.

"I'm growing a second personality," I say with a mouthful of egg and cheese.

Breakfast at the station is one of the few things that can make the god-awful wake-up time worth it. We eat at the kitchen island, surrounded by chipped mugs, a stack of overdue shift reports, and a fire pole that hasn't been polished in five years.

That's not a euphemism, by the way. I mean it literally hasn't been wiped down by anything other than sweaty man junk in ages.

As the crew settles into the day, Trevor nudges my arm. "So? Wednesday? You in?"

I chew, considering. I don't love bars. Sticky floors, fake flirting, shouting over music. But I also haven't been out in months, and I know Trevor won't shut up until I say yes.

I nod. "Yeah. Wednesday."

The bar Trevor drags us to on Wednesday night is exactly what I expected. Dim neon signs, a jukebox stuck in a cycle of country-rock and Nickelback, and that familiar tang of cheap beer and old regret. It's like every bar in every southern rom-com, just lacking the main characters. One thing about this small town is that we're all equals here, and at least seventy-five percent of the town's population has gotten blackout drunk in this very building.

We grab seats at the bar top. It was a quiet shift for once. One car accident, no fires, no major trauma. A blessing for the community, but it also means we're more restless than usual. Trevor keeps elbowing me to check out the women on the dance floor.

They're all beautiful, but none of them... hit.

They're loud, confident, drinking fruity cocktails with paper straws. They command attention, and they get it. Jackson's already practically levitating with excitement. These are his people.

Me? I'm watching like an outsider. Like I showed up to a party I wasn't invited to, but no one knows how to tell me to leave. I sip my beer, lean back, and wonder what it would feel like to walk into a room and spot someone who just gets me. Someone who doesn't require the sales pitch, the flirting, the charade.

Someone *real*.

I want to come home and kiss my girl on the forehead, not the mouth. I want a woman who starts crying at two a.m. because she dropped her fries on the kitchen floor and then laughs about it five seconds later. I want a wife who will nag at me when I put the pillows on the bed two inches too far to the left and accidentally leave a dozen mints in my pockets when I throw them in the wash.

The idea of finding that person in a bar like this? Feels about as likely as a cat saving a firefighter from a tree.

But then the door opens.

And suddenly, I'm eating my words.

She walks in with a subtle sway, her hoodie pulled halfway up her forearms, salmon-pink scrub pants just visible underneath. She doesn't scan the room. She doesn't seem to care about the attention. She just walks straight to the bar, orders her drink, and sips it like it's the only good thing that's happened to her all day.

And I *know*.

That's her. That's the woman I've been imagining in every empty bed, every quiet moment, every holiday, and every damn day.

Jackson follows my gaze. "You good?"

I don't answer. I can't. Because everything around me has gone quiet except her.

God help me, I think I just saw my happily-ever-after walk into a bar with sticky floors and a broken jukebox.

Chapter 2 | Venus

I never believed in love at first sight.

Not until I wandered into this bar, bleary-eyed, emotionally gutted, on the verge of tears, and saw the words *'Double Vodka Raspberry Lemonade'* written in curly pink chalk above the bar. In that moment, it felt like the only thing in the world that made sense.

The whole room smells like stale beer, and it normally doesn't bother me, but tonight it does. Everything does. The music's too loud, too; some early 2000s country song with a steel guitar that keeps scraping across my brain like a dull scalpel. The pool tables are too crowded, and I'm not even interested in playing pool.

I slide into an empty corner of the bar top and shrug out of my hoodie. My salmon-pink scrubs are still wrinkled and damp at the cuffs. I should just go straight home. I should shower and curl under a blanket. But the thought of facing the silence in my apartment feels louder than this place ever could.

The bartender, a baby-faced kid who probably just turned twenty-one, wanders over. His name tag says 'Noah.' He gives me a smile that doesn't reach his eyes.

"I'll take the vodka lemonade," I say.

He nods, pours, and slides the glass over. "Rough night?"

I stare at the drink for a second before nodding once. "Yeah. Something like that."

He doesn't press. Just takes my cash and leaves me alone.

I take a sip, then another. I close my eyes and let the burn trail down my throat like a punishment. I need to feel something other than the loop that's been playing in my head since the hospital. CPR compressions. A mother's scream. The cold, still weight of a newborn.

I whisper to myself, "I lost a baby today."

My voice cracks in the middle of the sentence. My hands start to shake, so I press them flat against the bar top like that'll hold me together. A single tear breaks loose and slides down my cheek.

It's my first loss.

I always knew it would happen eventually. The labor and delivery room is beautiful, yes—but it's also brutal. Birth doesn't always equal life.

Sometimes, it means grief in the shape of a tiny blue body and a soundless delivery room.

Everyone told me it wasn't my fault. The nurses, the OB, even the mother, in between her sobs. But that doesn't matter, because I was the one who held that baby and begged it to breathe.

I remember the wailing mother behind me. Her hoarse voice. Her hands clutching instinctively at nothing. I remember someone trying to pull me away, telling me it was over. But I didn't want to believe them. I didn't want to let go.

And now I can't let go of any of it.

I pick up my drink again. *Sip. Breathe. Sip. Breathe.*

The seat beside me shifts. I don't look up. Not until a soft, cautious voice says, "Hi."

I turn my head and find a man leaning against the bar—tall, confident, a little unsure of himself. His hair is golden-blond and his eyes are soft green, like leaves at the end of summer. There's a half-smile on his face that feels... safe. Not smarmy. Not performative. Not overbearing.

"Hi," I say. My voice is thick from crying, but he doesn't seem put off. In fact, he looks surprised that I spoke.

His smile grows. "I just... uh..." he laughs, embarrassed. "I had to come over and tell you that I think you're beautiful." He reaches for my hand and places a chaste kiss to my hand. Weird, but again, somehow not threatening.

I blink at him. Most guys don't lead with sincerity. They lead with cheap lines and the not-so-subtle threat of their presence. But he stays planted where he is, his hands clasped, his eyes level with mine.

"Thank you," I say.

He gestures toward my drink. "Can I buy you another?"

I shake my head. "No thanks. I'm at my limit."

"Lightweight, huh?" he says gently.

I study him. His posture is open but not imposing. His voice is warm but not trying too hard. My eyes flick to his hands. Calloused. Strong. His smart watch sits a little too high on his wrist, revealing a tan line.

"No," I say. "Just... had a rough day. Needed to feel something other than sorry for myself."

His smile falters. "I'm sorry."

From the corner of my eye, I spot two men across the bar, both tall and built like him, watching us with matching expressions of hopeful amusement.

I tilt my head toward them. "Your friends look like they're rooting for you."

He glances at them, then shrugs sheepishly. "Ignore them. They think they're my wingmen." He offers his hand. "I'm Carter. But my friends call me Vulcan."

I raise a brow. "Vulcan?"

He shrugs again. "It's a long story. Firehouse nickname. You know...Vulcan, the Roman God. Fire, steel, destruction... very flattering stuff." He shimmies a bit further into the bar and relaxes his stance. "Okay, so no drink this time. How about next time?"

I pause. There's something endearing about the way he's trying. Like he's both confident and a little out of his depth. It makes me want to be kind to him, but I can't let that turn into something. I don't have the room for anyone else's fire right now.

"Are you asking me on a date, Goldilocks?"

He grins. "Yeah. I am."

I give him an apologetic smile. "Sorry, but no thanks. I wasn't here to...anyway, I just...I should go home."

He nods, no pressure in his expression. "Okay." I grab my purse and slide off the stool, but before I reach the door, he calls out, "Wait!"

I stop, one hand on the handle.

"What's your name?" he asks.

I smile faintly. "Bye."

And then I'm gone.

Chapter 3 | Vulcan

"...and then he didn't even get her name!"

Jackson is practically wheezing with laughter as he slaps Trevor's back and doubles over, tears in his eyes.

Trevor's leaned halfway across the common room couch, reenacting my bar interaction with an invisible ponytail and the most dramatic impression of me I've ever seen. "'Uh, hi, you're beautiful, can I buy you a drink?' *Insert tragic rejection and walk of shame here.*"

I glare at both of them from the lounge chair in the corner, arms crossed like a pissed-off dad at a Little League game. "Are you done?"

"Not even close," Jackson says between gasps. "You got full-on rom-com rejected, my guy. She walked out without giving you her name like a sexy Cinderella and left you holding your—"

"Dignity?" I offer.

"Beer," he finishes. "She left you holding your beer."

"That doesn't even make sense," I huff.

I shake my head and try to tune them out, but it's no use. The image of her in that hoodie and those scrubs is already tattooed across the backs of my eyelids. And her soft, worn-out voice has been stuck in my head for days.

Even if our only conversation was a long winded rejection.

It's been four nights. *Four.* And I'm still thinking about a woman who gave me absolutely nothing to go on.

Just enough of an impression to haunt me. But, like, in a good way.

"She didn't seem creeped out, right?" I say aloud before I can stop myself, interrupting their banter.

Trevor raises a brow. "Dude, you kissed her hand. What was that? 1940's foreplay?"

"She looked sad," I mutter, as if that explains everything.

Jackson quiets down a little. "Yeah," he says, thoughtful now. "She did."

Before I can spiral into another round of self-inflicted overthinking, the department alarm shatters the mood. The lights in the station flicker red, and the sharp buzz triggers a switch in all of us.

Engine One respond. Major vehicle collision with confirmed fire. I-16 eastbound. Semi-truck involved.

Our Captain's already calling out roles as we move. I toss aside my water bottle and sprint for the bay. The others do the same, and within seconds, we're suiting up and loading into Leroy—our beat-up, beloved engine.

"Jesus, Westwood," Rodriguez says as I clip my radio in place. "Are you sure you're not an arsonist?"

I raise my hands in surrender. "Hey, I've got an alibi. You saw me getting roasted by my own wingmen just now."

Laughter fades fast as the doors open and Leroy pulls out into the street, sirens screaming. There's nothing like the feeling of being inside that engine. Adrenaline pounding. Heart thumping in time with the siren. The air charged with purposeful tension.

We hit the highway fast. Smoke is already visible on the horizon, thick and black against the early dusk. My fingers flex around the shoulder strap of my oxygen tank. This is what I do best. The chaos. The fire. The mission.

This is why I'm Vulcan.

We pull up to the wreck. It's bad.

The semi is jackknifed across two lanes, the cab completely engulfed. One sedan is crumpled behind it, but no extraction needed. The occupants were able to escape their vehicles before the fire started. EMS is treating them for minor cuts and scrapes. They'll take care of the people.

But the blaze? That's ours.

Rodriguez barks orders. We move fast.

Trevor hands me the nozzle. Jackson is on backup. I check my tank, my gear, my gloves.

And then we move. Stepping toward the flames in perfect synchrony, the heat instantly presses against me like a wall. The sound fills my ears. The roar. The crackle.

The pop of something collapsing inside the wreckage. My mind narrows into a tunnel. One task at a time. One move. One target. One purpose.

We work in unison, voices crackling through radios, boots pounding wet asphalt. The water hisses and explodes violently as it meets diesel-fueled fire. Steam clouds our vision. My arms burn with strain, but I keep going, because I can't stop.

This is who I am when I'm not sitting in bed wishing I had someone to kiss goodnight.

When it's over, the wreck is reduced to char, ash, and soaked black metal. We do a quick debrief with the Captain and the PD. We do a massive game of rock-paper-scissors to decide who has to write the report.

Jackson claps a hand on my back. "You good?"

"Yeah," I grunt. But my legs ache and my brain's still stuck on that quiet corner of the bar and the way that girl didn't look at me like I was a hero. Just a guy.

We head back to the station, the cab quiet except for the low hum of exhausted breath and the radio static fading into nothing.

Later, after we've checked gear and logged reports, I find myself in the kitchen. I wash dishes while Trevor sweeps behind me, as is tradition. We don't talk much, just the occasional crack about how we smell like burnt bacon and Monster.

"Wanna hit the bar again this week?" Trevor asks eventually. "She might come back. Maybe she's local."

"If she were, we'd have seen her at County," I say, drying a mug that somehow always ends up in the back of the cabinet. "We've been there enough lately."

"Maybe she works on a different floor. Somewhere you meatheads never go."

He's probably right, but I don't want to chase ghosts through hospital wings. That feels desperate. And I've already got one foot in the *'sad guy still thinking about a girl from a bar'* category.

I mutter something about being tired and disappear into the dorm. The cot creaks as I sit down, shoulders slumped, back burning from the work. I stare up at the bunk above me, but I'm not really looking.

I'm thinking about that girl. Gorgeous. Distant. Maybe I'm not willing to go chasing ghosts through the county hospital, but I'm willing to hold out hope that I'll see her again.

Jackson slips into the room a minute later. He sits on the bunk near my feet and nudges my boot. "You good?"

"Just thinking."

"About the girl?"

I don't answer. He doesn't press.

Eventually, I say, "Sometimes I feel like Vulcan's my only achievement. Like I'm just a collection of turnouts and trauma calls. And at the end of the day, I go home to no one. What's the point of being the hero if there's no one to come home to?"

Jackson nods slowly. "You're not even thirty, man. You've got time to figure that out. And, if you want my brutal honesty, maybe stop hoping someone will see you as a hero. Carter is good enough on his own."

I look over to him. "I think that might be the nicest thing you've ever said to me."

He scoffs. "Don't get used to it."

He leaves me alone again. I lie back, eyes closed, letting the silence settle over me. And even in that darkness, all I can see is that beautiful blonde hair.

Chapter 4 | Vulcan

Cheap beer. Sweat. Stale peanuts. Ah, the smell of a good time.

Schooner's is the only bar in town, and judging by the crowd, it's also the epicenter of every bad decision ever made in Terracotta, Georgia. You could probably carbon date the bar stools and find DNA from every high school reunion in the past thirty years. You never know what you're going to find in here, even if I was sipping beer just a few days ago.

I step inside and immediately feel the heat and noise settle into my bones. There's that low thrum of country rock vibrating the floorboards, pool balls cracking in the back corner, and the subtle, but unmistakable, whiff of spilled Fireball and cheap cologne. Every booth is full. Every stool is sticky. It's like nothing ever changes here.

Trevor and Jackson are already at our usual spot near the pool table. Trevor's halfway into a story, motioning to his pants and singing *'here comes the planeeeeee'*.

I don't even want to know what the context is.

"Cooter!" Trevor shouts, lifting his drink like a Viking. "You showed! Jackson owes me ten bucks!"

"Didn't think you'd actually come," Jackson says with a smirk. "Thought you might be off writing sad poetry about your mystery girl."

I give him a deadpan look. "Only on Tuesdays."

I drop onto a worn-out stool, the vinyl cracking under my weight, and sip my beer while my eyes sweep the room. I know it's stupid. There's no real reason to believe she'll be here. But I look anyway. Every time the door opens, my heart kicks up a notch.

The first few times, it's just wind. A few college kids. A woman I definitely went on a date with two years ago who still glares at me like I stole her dog.

No sign of *her*.

Jackson elbows me. "You sure she's not a ghost? Did we all just agree to your collective hallucination to protect your fragile man-heart?"

I ignore him. Mostly. But part of me does wonder.

Did I imagine the connection? The look in her eyes? Did I see what I wanted to see in that moment? Am I so desperate to find the one that I put that hope on the shoulders of the first girl who caught my eye?

The jukebox switches tracks. Something slower, heavier. The crowd shifts with the rhythm. I take another sip, just as the door creaks open again. At first, it's just a blur of movement. Then... her.

Yeah. That's her. No mistaking it.

She slips in behind a cluster of girls and doesn't immediately scan the room. Her hair is down this time— loose waves with streaks of gold that catch every pulse of neon light. She's not in scrubs tonight. Instead, she's wearing faded denim shorts and a pale yellow crop top knotted at her waist, the sleeves rolled high enough to show the freckles on her forearms.

Her boots thud against the floor like they've danced here before.

Trevor follows my line of sight and whistles low. "There's your girl," he says, as if my eyes aren't already glued to her.

I can't look away. She's got a different energy tonight. Last time, she was wilted. Hollow.

Tonight, she walks like she knows exactly where she is and who she's about to make nervous.

Me. She's about to make *me* nervous.

Jackson smirks. "Well, are you gonna talk to her or just drool like a feral golden retriever?"

I stand, brushing my hand over my shirt. "I'm going."

"Smooth like sandpaper," Trevor calls after me.

The crowd parts just enough to let me cross toward the bar. She's just ordered two drinks, one in each hand, and when she turns around, she spots me instantly. Her gaze doesn't flinch.

She gives me a smile. Teasing. Almost suspicious.

I lean over the bar like I did that night and try to mirror her smile. "Can I buy you that drink tonight?"

She arches a brow. "Vulva, right?"

"Vulcan," I correct with a grin. "Still hoping to hear your name."

"I don't give that out to strangers."

I nod, playing along. "Alright. Can I at least dance with you?"

She considers. Doesn't say yes. Doesn't say no. Just... walks away with a drink in each hand.

I blink.

She disappears into the crowd with the drinks, and I feel like someone just pulled the rug out from under me.

She's dancing now. Not wildly, and not for attention. Just a slow, deliberate rhythm that dares me to follow. Her hips sway, her hair brushes against her back, and every once in a while, she looks over her shoulder.

And catches me watching.

Again.

And again.

Each time she meets my eyes, I feel that heat in my chest spread—like fire licking up my ribs. She's doing it on purpose. She wants me to come to her.

Or she's playing with me.

Either way, I'm toast.

When I finally move, I don't walk. I stalk. Not aggressive. Just... pulled. Like gravity shifted and now she's the center and I'm completely caught in her orbit.

I reach her just as she spins toward the jukebox. We're tucked behind a booth, half in shadow. The air back here smells like sweat and perfume and spilled rum.

I lean in just close enough to speak. "What's your name?"

She gives me that maddening, unreadable smile again and traces a slow figure-eight with her hips. She doesn't answer. Just keeps dancing.

I hold back, not wanting to come on too strong. She's calling the shots, and I'm not stupid enough to miss that. It's hot, and I'm into it.

So I step back. Shimmy a little. Invite her in.

She laughs, just a little, and takes the bait.

We dance.

And it's—God, it's something else.

Her fingers brush my arm as she spins. Her hips sync with mine like we've done this before in another life. She's sweating a little. I'm sweating a lot. Her laughter catches in my shirt. My hands drift to her waist, careful, asking for permission with touch alone.

She lets me. Moves deeper into my touch. Four songs pass, and I'm breathless. Not from the dancing, but from her.

She tugs me toward the bar again and plops down on a stool like she owns it. I stand behind her, resting one hand on the bar, the other still tingling from where it held her waist.

"Can I buy you a drink?" I ask again.

She finally nods. "Just one."

I order a beer. She gets a vodka lemonade.

"You're a firefighter, right?" she asks, eyeing the logo on my hat.

"Yeah, you remembered," I confirm gleefully. "Hence the Vulcan thing. What about you? What do you do when you're not dancing circles around me on the dance floor?"

"Labor and delivery nurse."

I blink. "Seriously?"

She nods, stirring her drink. "Twelve-hour shifts. Crying babies. Boobie milk."

A lightbulb flicks on in my brain. The scrubs. The tears. The haunted look in her eyes that night.

"You were having a bad night last time," I say quietly.

Her smile fades a little, but she nods. "Yeah."

I hesitate, then say, "You didn't want to be seen then. But you let me see the redness in your eyes. You didn't tell me to fuck off."

She looks at me for a long moment. "You didn't feel like a threat. That was... rare."

My heart stumbles a little at that.

We fall into silence for a few seconds, just sipping. It's not uncomfortable. It's... quiet. Safe.

"So can I get your name now?" I ask.

"Nope," she says, smirking.

I clutch my chest dramatically. "Tragic. I guess I'll just have to give you one. I'm thinking...Venus."

"Like the *planet*?"

"Like the Roman goddess. You know, beauty, fertility. Seems fitting."

She raises her drink to mine. "To Vulcan and...Venus."

I give her a sly smile. "Did you know Vulcan and Venus were close in mythology?"

She leans in close. "How close?"

I lean closer. "Let me take you out and you can find out."

She nips my earlobe. "How about you just show me tonight?"

And just like that, I'm *fucked*.

Chapter 5 | Vulcan

The second we step into my apartment, clothes start flying. First it's my shirt, then it's her boots, then it's my belt. I'm unwrapping her like a birthday present and God, she's beautiful.

I skillfully flick off her bra and all she's got left is her pretty lace thong. She's not like other girls I've been with, where she hides her body away from me with insecurity. She's bold and clearly proud of her curves, guiding my hands to touch her in all the right places. Her breasts, her hips, her ass. As I grip and squeeze, my other hand slides down the front of her panties, searching for that sensitive spot between her legs.

The moment my calloused finger touches her clit, she rises up on her toes, trying to get my touch even deeper. She hisses and bites my lower lip when I easily slip a finger into her wet heat. She's dripping for me, and without abandoning my task, I lead her through my apartment to my bed.

I pull my fingers free and shove them into my mouth, getting the first taste of this goddess that's ended up in my bed. She tastes so fucking sweet, like fresh honey. My dick twitches when she takes the liberty of removing her underwear and spreading her legs for me.

When I kneel to taste her fully, she wastes no time in gripping my hair and pulling me closer. She rides my face like I'm a rodeo bull, and I trace my hands up her body to squeeze her perfect tits and play with her pretty pink nipples.

She moans as she bucks against my face, and I can't help it when I take one hand to stroke myself because if I don't I might whimper like a touch-starved virgin.

She yanks on my hair so rough that it pulls my face away from her center. She makes direct eye contact with me and demands: "Fuck me."

Yes, ma'am.

I fumble for a condom in my nightstand, rip it open with my teeth, and slide it on my shaft. I line myself up with her opening and shove in. Both of us groan together, and I use the headboard as leverage as I slam into her.

Watching her breasts jiggle and hearing her moan my name has me already wanting to bust, but I'm going to give this girl the best performance of my life.

"Harder," she says, but she's not begging, she's commanding.

Jesus, I'm already railing her as hard as I can, but I'll never back down from a challenge. I adjust my position, planting my foot on the ground and pressing her legs towards her chest until she's damn near folded in half like a pretzel.

"Oh, God, I'm close," she moans.

She's dripping onto my sheets and I don't even care. All I can think about is unloading into this girl and then cooking her breakfast.

"Oh yeah? You want to come?"

"Fuck, yes, come on, please."

My hamstrings are cramping, but I turn on turbo drive. Skin slapping skin fills my entire apartment and my headboard is slamming against the wall hard enough that it's chipping the paint.

The moment I feel her squeeze my dick and her legs start shaking, I lose it. Three more pumps and I seat myself as deep inside her as I can manage, filling the condom with my release.

I groan and catch myself with my hands before collapsing on top of her. She giggles slightly and unfolds her legs. It's the best sound I've heard all night.

When we both catch our breath, I flip to my side and then shift to my back next to her. I close my eyes and breathe in the sweet euphoria of a fresh lay.

My apartment begins to hum with the beginning of the upstairs neighbor's cha-cha slide. I turn to the blonde beauty with a dazed smile. Her spicy cherry perfume and the slight scent of her sweat cling to me and my sheets.

But she's already out of the bed and getting dressed.

She moves as if I'm not there, gathering her clothes and pulling on her jean shorts with ease. She's not exactly rushing, but it doesn't look like she's staying either.

She's...detached. After the night we just had? Detached?

Damn, was it really that bad to her? Ouch.

Trying to ease the building awkward tension, I ask, "Where's the fire?"

She smooths down her hair with her hands and smiles. "Nowhere! It's just time to head home."

"Already?" I ask, running my fingers through my own messy locks and trying to woo her with the flex of my bicep. Women like muscular arms, right? They have a thing for biting them, if the internet is to be believed. I glance at the clock on my bedside table. "It's not even midnight yet, Cinderella."

She shrugs. "Early morning."

I frown and sit up, trying to read her pretty face. "Uh...alright. But...can I see you again? I mean, I thought we had a good time." I say, trying to not let the sting apparent in my voice.

"We did!" she responds casually as if I didn't just fuck her brains out. "But it was just that...a good time. This isn't going to be a thing."

I raise a brow. "A *thing*?"

"It was great...really great." She grabs her boots and shoves her mismatched-sock-covered feet into them. She looks at me again and raises her own brow this time.

"Don't give me that sad hamster look. Haven't you ever heard of a one-night stand?"

With my thin sheets still covering my manhood, I stand up. "That's it then?" I ask, no longer trying to hide the sting of rejection.

"I didn't mean to give you the wrong impression if I did. But I'm not looking for a 'thing' right now."

"Ah," I say, finally understanding.

"Casual is just better for me." she says, as if how I feel means jack shit. But to be fair, we're strangers, so I guess my feelings rightfully mean nothing to her right now. She looks at me again and must read my thoughts. "Carter, you're great, but I'm not—"

"Looking for a thing. I got it."

Something like guilt or regret flickers in her eyes, but it's gone as soon as it appeared. She leaves my bedroom to head for the door.

In an attempt to stop her from just dismissing me outright, I hold the sheets around my waist and follow her to the front, but far enough away that I don't come off too strong. "Can I at least take you out sometime? A drink with no pressure?"

She pulls her small purse over her shoulder and shakes her head. "I don't think that's such a good idea."

"Why?"

She gives me that same seductive smile she gave me last night on the dance floor.

Damn she's beautiful.

"I don't want to lead you on anymore than I already have."

I shake my head. "You didn't. You haven't. I'm a big boy, you know. If it goes wrong after another night, then I'll leave you alone. And not to make it weird, but I think there really could be something between us."

She smiles again. "You're not making it weird, but I promise, you don't want this—" she motions down to her as if to point out flaws that aren't there. "—forever. Trust me."

My shoulders sag and I again try to ease the tension by making a self-deprecating joke. "My dick's that small, huh?"

She giggles and motions to the wet spot still on my sheets. "Yeah, I clearly had a bad time."

I nod in concession and give her my best charm. "Can I at least have your number? In case you want to have another bad time?"

She grabs the doorknob and opens it before turning over her shoulder. "No numbers."

"How about your name, then? I've been eight inches deep in you, I think a name is warranted. You know mine."

She tsks playfully. "Don't flatter yourself. Maybe six and a half." She looks up as if in thought. "Anyway...I think I like Venus better. Bye, Carter!"

She steps out into the breezeway and her laugh lingers in my ears. Soft...then it's gone. And so is she.

I stand in my doorway, still naked with the sheet slipping lower and lower on my hips.

I'm a little bit turned on.

But mostly confused as hell.

The first thing I do when I close the door is tear my apartment apart...searching for my tape measure.

Chapter 6 | Vulcan

The crew is finishing our rounds. The one and only fire station in the county is dimly lit while we test the lights and sirens of our beloved engine. We named him Leroy.

Yes, as in Leroy Jenkins.

Yes, we're idiots. How'd you know?

We've got the only engine in the county that's always rushing headfirst into dangerous (and not so dangerous) scenarios, so we needed to give him a fitting name.

We all head back upstairs to the lounge, and I lean against the edge of the pool table in the rec room while I wait for Jacks to take his shot. He and Trevor are nursing cold cans of Coca-Cola while I chug a Monster. We're all a little tired. We tend to get this way at the end of our 96-hour shifts. Half alive. Hungry. Sometimes even delirious from the boredom.

"So let me get this straight," Trevor says with a look of pure mischief. "You had a night in the sheets with the hottest blonde in the county, you still haven't gotten her name, *and* you fumbled getting her number? All those nights with your right arm really did it in for you, huh? Cooter can't last a second in a cooter."

I glare. "Do you want this can thrown at your forehead or your throat?"

Trevor shrugs. "Surprise me."

I throw my empty can at his head. "Please shut up."

"Okay so you're not a three-pump chump." Trevor continues. "Did you scare her off with your personality then?"

This time, I gently toss the pool cue at him, hoping it knocks him over the head, but he sacrifices the last of his coke to catch it.

"I'm just fucking with you, champ." Trevor says.

"Seriously though," Jackson interrupts Trevor from continuing to hear himself talk. "She works at the hospital, right?"

I nod. "Yeah, labor and delivery."

"So next time we're in the ER, just ask around like a lost puppy looking for his owner. This is a small town, somebody down in Emergency's gotta know her."

They joke, but I've actually considered it. She might feel differently about that night, but she wasn't just a fling to me. There was something more there. I can just feel it.

In my heart, not my dick.

Although my dick did enjoy itself.

Before I continue *that* train of thought, the shrill wail of the alarm fills the station. We all jump to our feet. Testing done. Adrenaline takes over. Training kicks in.

Residential structure fire. Heavy smoke and visible flames. Engine One respond.

The dispatcher's description of the fire focuses us further. I take the radio and confirm we're on our way as the Captain tells us to move. The last of the crew hops on the truck as it pulls out of the garage, and it's all lights and sirens on the way.

The ride is fast and tense. The crew takes turns checking each other's turnout gear and air tanks to ensure we're ready to go as soon as we reach the site.

We stare out of the window and watch the streets race by, each one of us knowing that our job is to be faster than the flames.

The smoke can be seen well before we reach the house. It's a small single-story on the edge of town, and it's completely engulfed already. Flame shoots out of the front door and broken windows. Thick black smoke curls and puffs into the sky like the devil himself is using the home as a cigar. The orange glow of the flames light up the street ominously as people from town begin to gather to watch the grim sight.

Captain Rodriguez shouts orders as we roll to a harsh stop. The hose is deployed and the protective gear is on.

Out front, our station's ambulance stops near the elderly couple as they watch their lives reduce to black ashes in the flames. The woman cries and the man is frantically pointing to the house, his shouting unintelligible over the loud flames.

Over the radio in our helmets, I hear Captain say their pet is still inside. A small brown yorkie.

I'll be damned if I don't find that dog. I start moving towards the house with Jackson at my back before they even finish describing where the dog was last seen in the house. With my brother covering me, we crawl through the house below the smoke. We hear a small, faint, panicked yapping on the far end of the main living area.

I squint through the smoke and see two small ears and a shaking little dog on a chair that looks more flammable than gasoline.

"Gotcha!" I breathe, reaching for the terrified yorkie as it yelps. Jackson leads me out of the house backwards on our hands and knees with his hand on my ankle. When we emerge from the house and the elderly woman sees her precious pup in my arms, she gasps and reaches for him.

All things considered, he looks fine. A bit of burnt fur but no concerning breathing patterns.

When I emerge into the night air, I pass the shaking dog into the arms of his owner. She gasps like I've handed her a newborn.

Oh God. I shouldn't have said newborn. Now I'm thinking about—

"Oh, Charlie! Oh, my baby, he's okay! Thank you, thank you—"

Her voice cracks, and her husband chokes up beside her. I take off my mask and give them a tired smile and motion to the small patch of singed fur on the pup's hind legs. "Take him to the vet just to be safe, alright? He's a tough little guy."

The woman clutches my hand, her palm warm and trembling. "God bless you," she whispers. I nod and join the rest of the crew attempting to get control of the inferno.

It takes hours, but the flames are finally dispelled. We're covered in sweat, soot, and water, and the house is a total loss, but the important part is that there were no casualties. The one thing about this town is that the community will come together to help out the couple that's lost everything.

We're four hours past shift change, and we're all toast. We're all exhausted. We smell disgusting. We're hungry. As we reach the station and change, I find myself unable to get off the bench in the locker room.

My elbows rest on my knees and I close my eyes, relaxing my back and trying to ease the tension there.

But it's not the fire that's got me worked up anymore.

It's that damn girl. Venus.

I can't help it. I know she probably forgot about me the second the post-nut clarity kicked in, but I haven't stopped thinking about her for even a minute.

No name. No number. The only thing I have to go on is that I know she works in the maternity ward at the hospital. I could go there and try to catch her on a break, but the more I think about it, it starts to sound more stalkerish than romantic.

I know a few nurses in the ER...maybe one of them knows her. But would that be even weirder if I asked?

I rub my face and eyes to try and get that golden hair out of my mind.

Does she really not want to see me again? Could I really be infatuated with a woman who has no interest in me?

It was so...sudden. I've never had a fling, even a one-night stand, leave so suddenly after a night in bed. It was almost like it meant nothing to her at all.

And I can't even be upset if it did, because who am I to her except the guy she met at the bar? She doesn't owe me anything.

"Great work with that dog tonight," Jackson says, nudging me on the way to his locker.

"Thanks," I grunt.

"Are you good?" he asks.

I shrug. "Have you ever met someone and been so sure that there was meant to be more?"

He chuckles softly. "Still caught up on this girl? Damn. It must have been a great night."

I shake my head. "It wasn't just the sex. I can't really explain it."

He pats me on the shoulder. "I know, bud. I'm sorry it didn't work out. Sometimes people come into your life for a second and shake everything up. Doesn't mean they're staying. Doesn't mean it wasn't real, either."

"I just wish I knew why, you know?" I say. "Like...what did I screw up? What did I say? Why was she so eager to leave?"

"Have you ever considered that she was telling the truth and that she just wasn't looking for anything serious? I know it sounds harsh but...maybe she really just wanted some fun. She works long hours like us. Sometimes you just need to take the edge off. I don't think she wanted you to take it so personally."

I sigh. "I know. I just need some time to let it go."

We're both dead tired and decide to end our conversation there. We say our goodbyes and head in separate directions. The weight of my exhaustion presses down on my eyelids as I drive home, but my mind doesn't slow down for one second.

When I finally slip into my apartment and fall onto the bed, all I can think about is my Venus. I know she's probably not thinking about me, but I hope she is.

But my last thought before sleep takes me, is that if I ever see her again, I won't let it be the last time.

Chapter 7 | Vulcan

Three weeks. That's how long it's been since I've seen Venus. Since she walked out of my bed, my apartment, and apparently my *life* without a name, a number, or a second glance.

I'm in my apartment, pouring a bag of chips into a bowl and pulling fresh-cooked burgers off the skillet. Trevor, Jacks and I are having a Sunday night football party.

Well, party is a loose term, since it's just the three of us. But burgers, beer, and football. Sounds like a good time to me.

But I'm pathetic, because I've been stuck in the cycle of thinking about Venus, and it's gotten to the point that I'm burning the burgers I'm trying to cook because my mind is elsewhere.

I just want to see her one more time. I've been back to Schooner's three times a week since I last talked to her, and it's like she's vanished.

No name. No number. Just a memory.

As I'm putting another round of burgers in the hot pan, Trevor and Jackson barge in together. Trevor drops two six-packs of beer on the counter and I give him a disappointed look. That is not enough beer to help me forget Venus.

I take one anyway, cracking it open with a bottle opener and chugging it. Trevor takes one next, slumping into one of my recliners in the front room. "Dude," he says as Jackson tosses two more six-packs on my kitchen counter. "This has to be some kind of record. Three weeks. That's a high-level simp. Olympic-tier. Gold medal for the USA!"

I roll my eyes, but he's not completely wrong. It is pretty pathetic, and long past due for me to move on. I flip the burgers then rest my hands on the kitchen counter. "So what do I do? Start swiping right again?"

Trevor grins. "Well there's this girl—"

I groan. "I do not want your seconds."

No offense to the girls he's been with, but there's just lines I don't want to cross with my friends. Sharing pussy is one of them. That mustache on his face is becoming a biohazard from how many women have sat on it. I want no part of that.

"She's a friend of a friend of a girl I hooked up with a few nights ago. She's seen you around. She's real cute and thinks you're cute. That's like...fate. How about I set you up?"

I shoot him an unimpressed glare. "Hard pass."

"Dude," Trevor protests. "I'm not saying you have to marry the girl. Just give her a chance. If you don't like her, then don't see her again."

The football game starts and we momentarily forget the conversation. As soon as it breaks to commercial, Trevor pulls up his phone and zooms in on a group photo of a group of girls.

He wasn't wrong, this girl is cute. Blonde hair, blue eyes, pretty smile.

But they're not *her* blue eyes and it's not *her* blonde hair.

But I also know I have to stop chasing the ghost of a girl that doesn't want me. Reluctantly at halftime, I agree to meet up with her. Trevor texts his fling and he passes along the girl's phone number. Her name is Evelyn, and I take a deep breath before sending a message introducing myself as a mutual friend and asking if she wants to meet me at the diner tomorrow night.

She replies quickly and enthusiastically.

I have to admit, it feels good to know that there's someone out there that's actually excited at the thought of seeing me, and Evelyn helps me forget about Venus.

For now.

I push open the door to the only diner in town. It hums with low conversation and a child asking their mom for a quarter so they can get a gumball at the machine by the register. My hands instinctively go into my pockets as I search around for a head of blonde hair.

I spy Evelyn just a few feet away. She waves and stands to greet me, giving me a sweet hug. She looks exactly like the photo, and her energy is adorable. The waiter comes to the table and we order, and then the conversation begins to flow.

She's great. Better than great. In fact, I'm enjoying myself. Most of the conversation is just getting to know little things about each other. Where we grew up. Our families. Our jobs.

She's a wedding photographer, and we laugh over the crazy stories of drunk wedding guests.

Just as my thoughts start to drift to the fact that Trevor might have been right about this, the door opens.

In the middle of one of Evelyn's stories about a bridezilla, my breath gets caught in my throat and my heart drops straight into my shoes.

It's her.

Venus.

The rest of the diner seems to fade into nothing. She doesn't see me, but I sure as hell see her. Same blonde curly hair. Same little jean shorts faded in all the right places. She walks in like she owns the floor tiles. Confidence in every line of her body.

She approaches the to-go counter and skims one of the sticky plastic menus there. She bites her lip and cocks her hip out as she considers her options, her ankle rolling in soft circles as she leans against the counter.

Then, like a slap, cold water splashes across my face. I gasp and the entire diner goes silent. I blink and regain my wits, looking forward to my date. Evelyn looks to Venus and then back at me, her face furious.

I open my mouth, but no words come out. Evelyn shakes her head, gathers her purse, and mutters 'jerk' as she storms out of the restaurant.

I sigh and take the last three limp napkins from the dispenser on my table to wipe my face. When I open my eyes again, a hand extends toward me with a few extras.

Venus gives me a teasing smirk. "She's better than me. I would've gone for the nuts."

Her causal tone makes me chuckle and I take the extra napkins from her. "It was deserved." I dab the wet spot on the front of my pants and slap the ice off my lap. "I didn't think I'd ever see you again."

"We live in a town with a population of six thousand people, of course we'd see each other around," she says.

"That's not what I meant." I say back. She takes a straw from the little container on the table and plays with the paper wrapper. "I meant that I wanted to...I just didn't think blindsiding you at the hospital was the best option. There's a very fine line between a romantic and a creep."

"Appreciated," she jests, poking me with the straw. "So, you looking for another hookup or what?"

I shake my head. "No!" I laugh out. "The exact opposite. I wanted to ask you on a date. A real one. Maybe one where I don't get waterboarded mid-salad." She raises a brow as if she doesn't believe me. "I'm serious. Don't get me wrong, that night was amazing and so is your body." I take the straw from her and poke her in the chest. "But I want to know the secrets you have in here, not just those secret butterfly tattoos on your hip."

"You've been holding out for weeks for a date with me when you don't even know my name?"

I shrug. "You said you like Venus better."

She sticks her straw and takes a sip of my own glass of water. She makes a dramatic sound like she's just quenched the greatest thirst. "Alright Goldilocks. Diner. Dinner. Date."

"You mean right now?" I ask.

Her food is ready and she unboxes a giant mound of cheese fries. She takes a plastic fork and points at them. "These don't travel well and I don't want to eat in my car."

Even though the water Evelyn splashed on me was ice cold, I feel like it couldn't be hotter in this diner. It must be her and the effect she has on me. I get nervous. She's giving me this chance and I don't want to fuck it up.

"So I got pooped on by a newborn yesterday," she says, as if that's a normal conversation to have at dinner, however run down the location might be. Maybe she's testing me to see if I can handle the gross stories she has to tell, but I'm a paramedic, and I've seen some things, too.

"I feel like that's a pretty normal occupational hazard," I say.

She laughs between a bite. "Yeah, but it was the most interesting thing that happened to me this week."

"Damn, and all I did was crawl into a burning building to rescue a puppy."

Her eyes widen. "Wait, really? You saved the dog, right? Tell me you saved it."

I smile. "Yeah, he was perfectly fine, just a little singed fur." I nod toward her. "You like dogs?"

"Everyone likes dogs! I want a pittie so bad, but my apartment doesn't allow dogs. As soon as I get a new place I'm hitting up the shelter though."

"You strike me as a golden kind of girl. Why a pit?" I ask.

"Why *not* a pit? They're adorable and they're just misunderstood. I've never met one that wasn't a total sweetheart."

As she finishes her fries, she goes on a long tangent about rescuing dogs and how if she wasn't a nurse she'd probably be a vet.

"So if you love animals so much, why'd you choose nursing instead? It seems like you're really passionate about animals."

She gives me an awkward smile that says the conversation is veering into territory that's not mine to tread in. "It's a long story."

She inhales through her teeth and gathers her garbage. She stands to leave, but I'm not letting her sneak out so easily this time.

"Wait," I protest, reaching for my phone and unlocking it for her. "Please, can I have your number?"

She looks at me like she's ready to say no, but after a long pause, she picks up my phone from the table and types in her contact info. When she hands me my phone back, I see that she's saved herself as '*Venus*'.

"That's not your name!" I protest.

"You asked for my number, not my name."

I huff but concede and stand with her. I lead her out of the diner and we say our goodbyes. Her exit isn't nearly as abrupt as our first meeting, waving to me over her shoulder and then again when she drives off.

You've got her, champ. Don't fuck it up.

Chapter 8 | Venus

The only sound in the delivery room is the rhythm of the fetal monitor and the tense breathing of a soon-to-be mother taking in as much air as she can between pushes.

"You're doing great, mama," I coo. "Just keep breathing and give me another good push."

She nods, tears streaming down her red cheeks. As most men are in the delivery room, her husband hovers over her looking like the baby is coming out of *his* body and complaining about how hard his wife is squeezing his hand during the most painful experience of her life. My eyes flicker to him, giving him a stern glare to hold it together. "Almost there, just keep holding her hand."

This has been a long labor. Mama opted to go through it naturally, so she's been in pain, moody, sometimes rude, but it doesn't bother me. This is one of those deliveries that makes me proud to be in this field. This couple has been trying to have a baby for years. They've been through everything. IVF, chemical pregnancies, miscarriages soon after getting the two lines they've been praying for.

They've been desperate, and anxious, for this entire pregnancy. Now that they're here, in the delivery room, moments away from meeting their first baby, all of that fades away.

These moments make me feel alive, and it helps me get over the grief of knowing I'll never have it myself.

As the doctor helps mama through her final pushes, I move to her side to coach her, but I do it almost on autopilot. My mind drifts to Vulcan. Carter.

He's a bit irritating, really, always lingering in my mind like the smoke he's so familiar with. He's sweet and charming, but respects my boundaries, which is a nice change from other men I've been with. He doesn't back down from my challenging teasing, and the push and pull between us is the most fun I've had in a long time. I think I like him, and that is a problem.

My thoughts come back to reality when I hear mama cry out for a final time. A blink of silence passes, and then the beautiful wail of a new life fills the room.

Mama sobs in disbelief as her new baby is laid gently on her chest. Her husband kisses her forehead and looks at his new son with pride and tears in his eyes.

This is the best part. Handing a baby to new parents so they can feel their tiny fingers and soft skin for the first time. It's a momentous time in life, like nothing else matters in the world except for what's happening in this delivery room.

I'll never experience that feeling myself, so I dedicate my life to giving it to others.

I help mama with her first feeding, and as they drift into that lovely little bubble of newborn bliss, I slip away to the breakroom.

I collapse into a chair and roll my shoulders as I pop some green grapes into my mouth as if I'll never eat again. You never know with this field, so we've all mastered the art of eating full meals in five-minutes flat.

I pull out my phone to check Facebook, when I notice a message from an unknown number.

Unknown: Miss me yet?

I furrow my brow and text back asking who they are. I see the typing bubble pop up, and my phone buzzes a second later.

Unknown: It's Carter. Have you already forgotten about me? Wow. Wounded.

Me: Sorry, I don't know any Carters. I only know Vulva.

Unknown: VulCAN.

Unknown: You didn't answer my question. Do you miss me enough to let me take you out?

Me: Depends. Do I get to throw water in your face?

Unknown: If you wanna get my face wet I know better ways.

I giggle to myself and roll my eyes before replying.

Me: Fine. But there better be snacks.

I shove my phone back into my pocket and finish my shift with a smile on my face.

Carter picks me up in his beat-up truck to take us to the drive-in movie theater. It's a pretty empty lot, so we get to come to a stop right in the middle of the screen to get the best view. The sky is streaked purple and blue from a fading sunset, and soon it will be filled with millions of glittering stars.

I'm wearing an old sweatshirt and a pair of leggings, with my hair pulled up into a high, messy ponytail. I told Carter to bring snacks, but I didn't trust him to get the right ones, so my mini backpack is filled to the brim with my favorites. Barbecue chips and black licorice.

When I pull them out of my bag, Carter's mouth falls open. "You like black licorice?"

"Yeah. Why? You think it's gross?"

He opens the center console of his truck and pulls out a bag of his own black licorice, popping a piece into his mouth. "You kidding? It's my favorite!"

I recline back into my seat and the drive-in employee delivers our order of popcorn, soda, and nachos to the truck. Carter looks like a man starved when he opens the lid of the nachos, only to lift one out of the box and painfully tell me they're not cheesy or jalapeño-y enough for him.

We've both seen the movie already, so instead of watching, we critique the bad acting and CGI effects from the early 2000's. It's the most fun I've ever had watching a shitty movie.

The cool autumn breeze drifts into the truck cab through the cracked windows. I lift my legs up to rest the feet on the dash and get more comfortable. I peek over at Carter, and he's focused on the screen, but he's also got this cute smile plastered on his face that shows off a dimple on his cheek. He pulls off his cap to brush some of his loose hair back before putting it back on backwards. His head drifts in my direction and he catches me looking at him. He gives me a knowing raise of his brow.

I raise my hands in surrender. "You caught me. Sorry, just...you have a nice smile."

He cocks his head as if it's the first time someone's complimented it. "Thanks."

"So are you really not going to ask why I've been playing hard to get?"

He shrugs. "If you wanted to tell me, you would. Maybe you just like the chase."

I shake my head. "It's not that at all. I like spending time with you, more than I probably should. But I'm not looking for–"

"A thing?"

"Yeah. I'm not looking for a thing. And you're great, so I don't want to mislead you about what this–" I motion between us, "–is."

"Who says we need to put a label on it? For the one who doesn't want this to be a thing, you seem pretty eager to slap one on it."

I give him a thankful smile for his understanding. "I just don't want you to think this is going somewhere that it isn't."

He sighs. Not in a defensive or hurt way. Just a sigh. "Venus, I just want whatever this is to be real. If that means shitty movie and licorice, I'll consider myself lucky."

"You're really okay with casual?"

"I mean...would I like more? Yeah, of course. But if that's all you're willing to give me, then that's enough for now."

I scoff playfully. "You're great, you know that? It's kinda suspect."

He laughs and turns back to look at the screen for a second. "Maybe you've just got low standards."

"Low standards, huh?" I ask as my hand drifts over the center console to rest on his thigh. My fingernails drift along the rough fabric of the taut denim on his thigh. "Where should my standards be, then?"

His breath hitches and he swallows slowly as he looks at my hand tracing patterns on his thigh. I shift closer as my hand rides upward.

"Here?" I ask, rubbing the bulge in between his legs. He lets out a shaky breath and bites his knuckles. "Use your words, Vulcan. Or can you not handle the heat?"

"Shit, yes, put me in your mouth."

He lifts his hips and shoves down his boxers, letting his full girth spring free. He sighs at the relief from the confines of his jeans. I wink at him and lick one thick stripe up his length, balls to tip with a flat tongue. He bucks his hips when I reach the spot on his shaft directly below the tip, so I swirl my tongue there until a fat drop of precum leaks from the head. I greedily lap it up.

I suck his shaft into my mouth and hollow my cheeks, I catch his eyes rolling back just a second before his head falls back to his head rest. His hand lightly grips my head and presses me down a little further. I gag a little, but take him all the way to the back of my throat before I let myself breathe.

I only take one deep breath before I dive back in, bobbing my head to the ever-increasing rhythm of my heartbeat. My spit drips out of my mouth, leaving a mess all over his crotch and my hands.

Carter uses both of his hands to pull my hair into a tight ponytail and holds my head still as he starts rocking into me. The salty taste of his precum fills my mouth, and then he grunts loudly before his warm release shoots into my throat. Some escapes, but I swallow what I can and lick my lips before lifting my head.

When I pull back, we're both breathing heavy. My lips are swollen and my hair is a mess. His eyes are wide with that post-sex haze men get, and he's got a lazy grin on his face as he tucks himself back into his pants and buckles his belt.

"If that's your casual blow job, V, I might not survive your committed one."

Chapter 9 | Vulcan

The past two days have been bombarded by text notifications blowing up my phone.

From Venus, you ask? Of course not. From the two idiots I call my best friends. The second I step into the station, I'm ambushed like I've got a fresh hickey on my neck and forgot to cover it.

"Alright, Romeo, fess up!" Jackson calls from the kitchen, already halfway into an everything bagel that looks suspiciously stale.

Trevor leans around the fridge door with that same smug face he had when he once convinced a girl that his mustache was genetic. "Did you kiss her? Did she slap you? Did you bang? Did you propose? Should we start looking for tuxes?"

I grunt and shove past them toward the coffee machine. I tear into a protein bar and bite it, speaking through the salted caramel flavor. "A gentleman never tells."

"Hey Jacks, is he blushing?" Trevor mutters. "This is why you need to grow a beard, man. It might preserve your dignity."

I'm trying not to smirk. I'm failing. My face is betraying me hard right now.

Because yeah, it went well.

Really fucking well.

But I'm not giving these two the satisfaction of hearing about it. Not yet. Not when I'm still trying to wrap my head around the fact that she texted me first this morning. A little heart emoji next to a *"Bring extra licorice next time."*

That's basically a love letter, as far as I'm concerned.

I head to the gym, needing to burn off the grin that's basically tattooed onto my face. Mid-bench press, my phone buzzes. I ignore it, thinking it's just a meme from Trevor about how *"true love is when she doesn't flinch at your morning breath."*

But then it buzzes again. And again.

Three messages. One from Venus.

I rack the bar with one hand and wipe my other on a towel before checking it. There, glowing against my cracked screen, is a photo that momentarily breaks my brain.

Red lace.

Venus: Help me, fireman. I seem to be stuck in my bra.

I stop breathing for a second. I forget that I'm in a room with fluorescent lights and the distinct smell of sweat and preworkout. I forget that I'm wearing socks that don't match and that this girl ghosted me just a few weeks ago.

Is she seriously flirting with me?

I look around the gym to ensure I'm alone and do a fist pump of victory to myself. I snap a photo of my gym shorts, very clearly showing the effect of that photo.

Me: On my way with the jaws of life.

Not five seconds later, the door to the gym swings open and Trevor strolls in, Jackson right behind him.

"You hogging the squat rack again, Grandpa?" Trevor asks, flinging his towel over his shoulder like a coach who never made varsity and vicariously lives through his son that barely made JV.

Jackson eyes me, squints. "Why do you look like you saw a ghost?"

Trevor leans over and whispers loudly out of the side of his mouth to him. "I think he just sexted one."

I grab a dumbbell to mask the absolute chaos in my pants and hope the pump pulls the blood from my groin. "Just thinking about last night."

Trevor raises a brow. "You know what they say about us men...we've got two heads but only enough blood to use one at a time."

We settle into our usual banter, but my mind is still spinning from her message. Not because it was risqué (though I'm not complaining) but because it was *her*. Reaching out. Playfully.

Willingly.

And that tells me more than any confession ever could.

Later, when the guys head upstairs to raid the kitchen for protein shakes that taste like chocolate-flavored drywall, I duck into the locker room and pull out my phone again.

Another picture. No face this time, just legs, bare and tangled in red silk sheets.

Venus: You're late. The fire's spreading.

I bite my lip, scroll back to her first message. The little part of my brain that does long division and knows how to file taxes? Gone. Torched. The only thought left?

This girl is gonna ruin me.

And I think I want her to. No, I take that back. I definitely want her to.

I type back, thumbs shaking just slightly:

Me: Whenever you want, I'll be there. Not just for the fire.

No photo this time. Just honesty.

Then I slide the phone back in my pocket and head toward the chaos of lunch, knowing that no matter what happens next, I'm not walking away from this fire.

Not unless she tells me to.

And I know I'm in too deep when that thought already devastates me.

Chapter 10 | Venus

The city skyline slips past the car window like we're fast-forwarding time, glass and metal flickering in the sunlight. Callie hums along to some girly-pop song I don't know, and I try not to think too hard about why I agreed to this little getaway.

That *'why'* is a six-foot-tall blond.

I need retail therapy. Girl time. Whatever distraction I can find today.

We're in the next city over. It's bigger, louder, and thankfully lacking in firefighters who've seen me naked.

Callie whips the wheel into a parking garage, and the sunlight cuts stripes across her face through the concrete slats. She parks, turns the engine off, and looks at me over her chic sunglasses.

"You've been suspiciously chipper lately," she says like she's been waiting until I'm trapped miles away from home to interrogate me.

I frown. "Huh?"

"You've been humming," she adds. "And smiling. And, this is the most damning evidence of all: you've been washing your hair."

I unbuckle my seatbelt with a roll of my eyes. "You're reaching."

She follows me out of the car with a smirk. "And don't think I haven't noticed how the shower drain has been clogged with your leg hair. We've been living together for three years, V, and you don't shave your legs for no reason."

Okay, she has a point.

We step out into the crisp morning air, crossing toward a row of boutique shops and overpriced coffee shops filled with granola moms. I link my arm through hers out of habit, our boots clacking against the pavement in time with a street musician's bluesy guitar.

"I'm not trying to pry," Callie says, even though we both know she absolutely is. "I just want to know what's got you walking around like you're in a tampon commercial."

I scoff. "That's offensive. I don't even use tampons."

"It's a metaphor, babe," she counters. "So...it's the firefighter, right?"

My stomach flips. I play it cool. "Carter? I mean, he's great, but–"

She stops mid-step. "Oh my God, you just called him Carter. You used his actual name. Not Vulcan. Not Vulva. You're *gone*."

I unhook my arm from hers and keep walking, irritation creeping into my cheeks. "It's not like that."

"V."

I pause in front of a boutique with a window full of bedazzled cowboy hats and glittery boots. "It's casual," I say, repeating the mantra I've been clinging to for weeks. "It's fun. He's just...easy to be around."

She raises an eyebrow. "Except for the part where he texts you good morning and shares your love for the worst candy known to mankind, and gave you a nickname after a Roman goddess."

I turn sharply to face her. "Stop being cute. This is not feelings. This is just... orgasms."

Callie grins like she's won. "So emotional support dick. Got it. I give it another month before you're planning the wedding."

I laugh despite myself and push open the boutique door. The smell of patchouli and overpriced linen hits us like a wall. We meander past a rack of upcycled denim before something catches my eye.

A dress.

It's fire engine red. Spaghetti straps. Short enough to tease. The kind of thing you wear when you want to be the only thing someone sees in a room. Callie follows my gaze and lets out a low whistle.

I grin. "It's cute, right?"

She tilts her head. "Planning to wear that on a real date with Carter?" She sings his name like she's mocking me on the playground at school.

"No," I say, but I don't make an effort to stop looking at it. Callie takes it off the rack and holds it up to my body and forces me to turn toward the mirror.

Callie gasps. "This looks like you're ready to ruin someone's life. And red for a firefighter? It was meant to be. You're going to be so smoking hot, he'll need backup."

I smirk to hide the blush in my cheeks, because she doesn't know about the red lace bra I bought specifically to wear for him. "I'm hoping he'll bring the *thick* hose."

Callie chokes on a laugh loud enough to startle a woman browsing handbags. "You're such a menace."

I carry the dress to the checkout and pretend it's not a symbol of anything. It's just a dress. For a man I'm not dating. Who I'm not catching feelings for.

Just a dress.

Later that night, I try it on in front of my mirror in the privacy of my room, twisting side to side to see the full effect. My phone buzzes on my bed with a text.

Vulcan: Any chance I can see you tonight?

My fingers hover over the keyboard.

Me: Depends. You bringing snacks?

He doesn't text back right away. I sit down on the edge of my bed and stare at the ceiling. This is stupid. I'm being stupid. I like the way he looks at me, like I'm the only thing in the room. I like...

Damn it.

Him. I like *him.* And I shouldn't. I can't.

The next buzz from my phone snaps me out of my spiral.

Vulcan: I'll bring the snacks.

I smile.

Me: I'll bring the dress.

Chapter 11 | Vulcan

I'm standing in front of my bathroom mirror staring at a bottle of cologne. I do a final check before stepping out of the bathroom. Pits, deodorized. Face, shaved. Pubes, trimmed.

Teeth? I smile into the mirror at myself.

Sparkling.

It's not a date. She wants casual. It's *not* a date.

But also... she bought a new dress. For me. For her. For us. Whatever *'us'* means to her.

Not that she told me that outright, but when she texted *'I'll bring the dress'* in response to my invite, I saw the little preview of a photo at the bottom of the screen.

It opened into the most dangerous thing I've ever seen: Venus, in red, in her bathroom mirror, biting her lip like she doesn't know she's the eighth wonder of the world—or at least the one I'm living in, and that's all that matters to me.

I splash cold water on my face and dry off before tugging on a clean black tee and jeans. I grab a plastic sack filled with the black licorice and barbecue chips before heading for the door.

The whole way to her place, I'm trying not to overthink it.

This isn't love. Not yet. Maybe not ever, if she's serious about not wanting anything real. But it's something. The way she looks at me makes me want to be her safe place, even if it's temporary.

By the time I pull up outside her building, the sky's turning purple, and there's that edge of chill in the air that confirms fall is fully settling in.

I knock twice. She opens the door with wet hair and no makeup. Barefoot. No dress.

For a second, I wonder if I got the night wrong. I pull out my phone and check. I laugh nervously. "Sorry, I must've gotten excited and got my dates mixed up."

"No, you didn't." Then she steps back, letting me in, and says, "Disappointed?"

"Never."

We settle on her couch, some old horror movie playing on the TV for background noise. She's in an oversized hoodie and curled up like a cat, one hand tucked under her cheek, the other digging through the snack bag like it's a stocking on Christmas morning.

"You remembered the licorice!" she mumbles, chewing with a soft smile.

"I remember everything," I say, watching her instead of the movie.

She gives me a sidelong glance. "That's dangerous."

"I'm a firefighter. I like danger."

"Danger, or adrenaline?"

She tosses a piece of licorice at me, and I catch it with my mouth. She pretends not to be impressed, but I catch her smiling when she thinks I'm not looking.

About twenty minutes in, her feet drift into my lap, stretching her legs. I rest my hand on her ankle, brushing my thumb back and forth. It's not sexual. Not entirely. Just comfort. A connection that doesn't need words.

She doesn't pull away.

Halfway through the movie, she breaks the silence. "You ever feel like something good is about to happen, so your brain starts making lists of all the ways it could go wrong?"

I pause. "Not really, I tend to be an optimist. Why?"

She raises a brow. "That's where I live, emotionally. Glass half-empty."

I shift to face her more. "Can I tell you something?"

She blinks at me. "Please don't say something profound. I'm already emotionally constipated."

I smile anyway. "I know you don't want anything serious. And I'm not here to pressure you. But if this thing between us ever stops being casual, I won't run. Just so you know."

She sits up, searching my face like she's trying to catch a lie before it escapes. She pulls her feet away from my lap, but the distance suddenly doesn't just feel physical. It's emotional, too. She's closing off.

"What if I do?" she asks.

"Do what?"

"Run."

"I won't chase you, if that's what you're worried about." I lean forward and tuck a piece of curly blonde hair behind her ear. "Instead, I'll wait right here. Until you stop running."

She doesn't say anything after that. Just leans in slowly and kisses me.

It's not the hungry, teeth-clashing kind of kiss we started with weeks ago. It's soft. Careful. Like she's testing shark-infested waters and she's got an open, bleeding wound.

I kiss her back, just as slow. Just as real.

When we pull away, her fingers are curled around the hem of my shirt, anchoring herself.

"Do you want to stay tonight?" she asks as she slowly lifts my shirt, and her voice is quieter than I've ever heard it.

"Yeah," I say, my hand moving to her thigh. "I really do."

She nods, pulling my shirt off and then her own. I unhook her bra and toss it to the side, sucking one of her nipples into my mouth as we help each other shed the rest of our clothes.

She's on my lap, wet pussy pressed against my aching cock, both of us trying not to move.

"You got a condom?" she asks, like she'd be devastated if I said no.

"Wallet," I answer breathlessly, and with her position on the couch, she leans over, digs through my pants that are discarded on the floor, and fishes my wallet from my pocket.

The wrapper is torn off in a millisecond and she slides it down my length like a pro, wasting no time lining it up with her center.

She's so eager, and the lack of foreplay makes the initial stretch so much slower and intimate. Little by little, she sinks onto my cock until I'm all the way in. She whimpers a bit when she feels the full length of me all the way inside.

With full eye contact, she begins to ride me like she owns me—and who am I kidding? She does. I let her fuck me in the way that feels best for her, grinding herself down hard enough that her clit brushes against my pelvis with each pass.

My eyes roll back in my head and my hands go to her hips when her walls start squeezing me, signaling that she's close. She begins to bounce higher, harder, and faster. Her beautiful tits bounce in my face, doing their own mesmerizing dance that has the male in me in a chokehold.

"Jesus, V, you're gonna make me cum," I warn her, feeling myself reaching that sweet edge.

"Not without me, you're not," she breathes out, her face twisted in the pleasure she's bringing herself.

"Oh yeah?" I challenge, tightening my grip on her hips and anchoring my foot to the ground. "Then let's get you there."

Without warning her, I snap my hips up at a brutal pace. Her moans die out into breathless, silent screams as the sensation takes over. She collapses into my chest, giving us a new angle to work with, and I keep up my brutal pace. There's a cramp forming in my hamstring but I don't care.

"Ah, Carter, I'm gonna—"

She doesn't even get to finish her sentence. I explode into her and she's right behind me, milking me with her silk walls until she's pulled my soul out of my body.

We're both spent, and I find myself wrapping my arms around her just a bit tighter as she catches her breath while lying on my chest.

I meant what I said, that I want to stay tonight.

But the thing I want more? Is for tonight to turn into tomorrow morning, and then tomorrow night. Then the next day. Then next week.

My heart hurts knowing that for her, our future won't extend that far, at least not in the way I want it to.

Chapter 12 | Venus

I wake up to the smell of laundry detergent and the steady rhythm of a heartbeat under my cheek.

For a second, I forget where I am. Who I'm with. Then I shift, feel the weight of his arm across my waist, and remember everything.

He's still asleep, mouth slightly open, one hand resting on my hip like it's always belonged there. And God help me, I like it. I like him. I like the way my apartment doesn't feel so chaotic with him here. Callie and I are always coming and going after long shifts, that this place feels less like a home and more like a hotel. But with him here, it feels more grounded. He fits perfectly in my bed despite it being too small.

This is not casual. It's quickly turning into more and I can't let it. He knows it because I told him, but I know it because I know me and the baggage I come with.

I can't do long term. It's not in the cards for me and I've made peace with that. Carter is a nice guy, and I don't want to play with his heart.

It's so obviously big and aching for love.

Love that I can't give him.

I slide out of bed carefully, trying not to wake him. My feet hit the cold floor as I shuffle into the kitchen, pulling his shirt down to cover my rear a bit more. It smells like him. Like cedar and soap and something warm underneath it all. I lift the fabric to bury my face in the collar for a second before shaking myself out of it.

Get a grip, V.

I don't do this. I don't feel things. Feelings are messy. They make me do irrational things, like plan your outfits for a man or get butterflies when I wake up next to him.

I brew a pot of coffee and try not to think about how he stayed. Not just physically, but emotionally, too. He didn't even flinch when I told him there was a chance I might run. He planted his feet and practically promised he'd wait for me.

And I know those weren't just empty words or a ploy to get in my pants. He meant it.

My phone vibrates on the counter with a text from my roommate and best friend.

Callie: So...did he bring the thick hose?

I roll my eyes and reply:

Me: He brought the whole engine.

Callie: Damn. I'm jealous. Think he's got any friends?

I laugh to myself and put the phone face down before grabbing two mugs from the cabinet. Behind me, I hear footsteps and turn to see Carter walking in, shirtless, rubbing sleep from his eyes like the small-town Roman statue he is.

"I was gonna bring you coffee in bed," I say.

He yawns. "And miss the chance to see you in my shirt? Not a chance."

I wrinkle my nose when he takes a sip of it with no cream or sugar. He sets the mug down and leans on the counter, his gaze warm and unreadable. "So... was last night okay with you?"

"Yeah," I say quickly. "It was good."

He studies me for a moment. "I didn't mean the sex...I meant me staying the night."

I study him back. "I asked you to."

He leaves that conversation there as if he's afraid pressing further will bite him in the ass. He takes another sip of his nasty bean water, then gestures toward the fridge. "Mind if I make something?"

"Be my guest."

He finds eggs, spinach, and a little leftover cheddar and starts cracking eggs like he's done it here a hundred times. Watching him move around my kitchen like he belongs here... it's domestic.

And dangerous. I shouldn't be letting him get comfortable here.

I exhale. "I'm not good at this."

"At cooking breakfast?"

"At...*things*."

He chuckles, but doesn't say anything back, inviting me to elaborate but not pushing the subject.

"I just don't want to lead you on," I add. "I don't want you to get stuck waiting for something that's never coming."

He sets the spatula down and turns to face me fully. "You don't owe me anything."

I blink. "Then why do you keep showing up?"

He shrugs. "Because I want to."

"But what if it doesn't turn into anything? What if it stays casual forever and you waste your time?"

He walks around the counter and stands in front of me, just close enough that I have to tilt my head to look him in the eyes.

"One day when you're ready, we'll talk about why you feel that way, and we'll figure out what that means for us. For now, how about we make a deal that whatever this is, it stays real?"

My throat tightens. I want to say something but nothing comes out.

Instead, I nod. He gives me a smile that assures me this is all good enough for him.

For now.

But will it be enough when he finds out how broken I really am?

Chapter 13 | Vulcan

If you had told me six months ago I'd be square dancing in the middle of town in front of half of Terracotta, Georgia while trying not to trip over my own boots, I would've said no way in hell.

But Venus loves dancing. It's how she lured me in that second time at the bar, and when we came back to this place and she saw an opportunity to outdance the entire town, it was on.

"Just follow my lead and they don't stand a chance," she says as we write our names on the sign up form. "Don't embarrass me and maybe you'll get lucky afterward."

I smile down at her, but she doesn't see it, distracted by placing her drink order at the bar.

"I'm already lucky," I whisper to her back. She looks over her shoulder at me, her eyes peeking out from my cowboy hat that she stole from me. Classic red flannel and criminally short shorts paint the rest of her.

"You nervous, big man?" she asks

"I run into burning buildings for a living, you think I'm scared?" I say to try and hide a gulp.

"You realize dancing requires rhythm, right?"

"I've got rhythm. I was born with rhythm."

She raises an eyebrow that says she's pressing 'X' for doubt, but she raises her drink to mine for a toast.

I spy Jackson and Trevor pointing at the sign-up table, and I know they've seen my name on the paper. We meet eyes from across the room and they scramble over to us.

"Cooter!" Trevor yells over the music. "You're cruel, man, giving your girl secondhand embarrassment from your suck-ass dancing skills."

"She's now been seen out in public with the three of us. What could be more embarrassing than that?" I tease down to her. She looks up at me and giggles, sliding under my arm and wrapping hers around my waist.

My hand slips into the back pocket of her shorts and I hold her close as we watch the other entrants hit the dance floor. By the time it's our turn, we might both be a little bit too drunk to actually make this good.

But I don't care. Neither does she. She's bouncing on her toes like she's having the time of her life.

"You ready?" I ask, holding out my hand.

She looks at it like I've handed her something dangerous. "Just don't step on my foot."

I give her my most charming smile. "Wouldn't dream of it."

The music starts, and the room erupts into a huge applause when we end up with the best song of the night: *Save a Horse (Ride a Cowboy)*.

Suddenly we're spinning, stepping, and laughing like we've done this a hundred times.

Venus is light on her feet. I fumble over and over, but she pulls me right back in each time like she's tethered to the beat itself. The crowd is clapping along, and someone yells my name when I manage to dip her without dropping her.

That part? I didn't rehearse. Pure instinct fueled by a little too much rye whiskey.

She gasps a little when I catch her just before her head hits the floor, eyes wide, mouth open.

And then she laughs like it's the best thing that's ever happened to her.

Nothing makes me feel more like a man who's got it all than hearing that sound come out of her.

"Careful," she whispers when I pull her back up. "You do that too well."

"Guess we're both full of surprises."

We keep dancing, even when we're clearly off the beat. At one point, we're barely doing square dancing at all. She breaks into a poor attempt at the robot, just to get a reaction out of me. She succeeds.

We're sweaty and out of breath by the time the final round finishes, and we come in third behind the elderly couple whose house burned down a few weeks ago. They moved like they were possessed by the ghosts of competitive dancers.

Fair.

Just kidding. That shit's obviously rigged, but for good reason. When they won, the entire bar donated to the prize pool fund to help them with rebuilding their lives.

"That was fun," Venus says, wiping sweat from her forehead as we collapse into a booth.

"See? You were so worried I'd embarrass you."

She eyes me. "Don't let it go to your head, Vulcan."

She leans back on the bench, looking up at the neon signs overhead. Her smile softens into something quieter. Content.

And suddenly, I want to ruin the mood by saying something honest.

I can't help myself. So I do.

"You make it really hard not to fall for you," I admit, with my head resting on my hands as I stare at her like a lovesick fool.

She freezes. Her entire body goes rigid. "Carter..."

"I'm sorry," I say, fast. "I'm not trying to scare you. But we promised we'd keep this real, right?"

She stares at me for a long moment, like she's trying to decide if this is the part where she runs.

Maybe she feels bad for me, because she does her best to relax.

"You should stop talking before you ruin it," she says. It sounds harsh, but I know she didn't mean it like that.

She's just protecting the parts of herself she's so convinced can't be happy. I get it, I do. But I'm more of a wear-my-heart-on-my-sleeve kind of guy.

Even if that means she might be the next one to break it.

Before I can open my mouth and ruin it some more, she grabs my arm and pulls me out of the booth and out of the door.

Chapter 14 | Vulcan

The second we step out of the bar, the air hits us like a wall—thick with the first taste of autumn clinging to everything it touches. The neon sign behind us gives one last flicker before fizzling out, like even it's too tired to pretend anymore.

We don't even make it half a block before Venus grabs my shirt and pulls me into her. And I mean *into* her, like she's afraid I'll start talking again and needs to make sure she shuts me up.

I kiss her back, memorizing the taste of lemonade and vodka on her lips, mixed with fruity ChapStick. She's delicious. Every bit of her. It makes me crazy for more.

"I live closer," I huff out between a nibble on my bottom lip. I might have been buzzed before, but I'm perfectly sober now. She says nothing, just follows my lead as we stumble towards my truck.

She nibbles on my throat, and I take that as the green light to stumble to my truck and lift her into the seat. The entire drive, I've got one hand on the wheel and one hand all over her. She's half naked by the time we get there and my belt is undone before I even shove the key in the front door lock.

We don't even make it to the bed. We crash to the couch. She lands on her back and I catch myself over her, all without letting her lips escape mine. Everything is a blur. Our remaining clothes are strewn all over the apartment, and my hands rest on her hips as I admire her body.

She doesn't give me much time though, because she grabs my dick like she owns it. I hiss when she gives it a squeeze and I reach for my discarded pants to find my wallet and pull out a condom. She keeps stroking me and makes it very hard to concentrate on getting it secured to me.

I take control of the situation again by flipping her over on her stomach and pulling her hips closer to me.

"Good girl," I whisper as she arches her back and wiggles her pretty little ass against me. I slip right into her with one easy thrust and she whimpers loudly. I pull out and thrust back in, starting a rough pace that doesn't seem to satisfy her.

"More, Carter. Please," she begs. She matches my rhythm by slamming herself backwards with each of my thrusts. I gather her hair into a ponytail in my fist and pull, giving myself enough leverage to fuck her harder.

An empty glass on the table next to the couch gets knocked off from the vibrations, shattering all over the laminate flooring. It only encourages me to go harder. I want this entire apartment to be a bigger mess than Venus when I'm through with her.

I'm railing her as hard as I can manage. This is not the kind of sex we normally have. This is more primal, more urgent. Everything I've been holding back is shoved into each thrust, and I know she can feel it, even if she'd never admit it.

The alcohol has been burnt out of my body by the adrenaline rush I get being with her. I'm perfectly sober, all of my thoughts consumed by this girl and whatever I have with her, desperately trying to fuck my feelings into her heart because for now, it's the only thing she responds to. I can feel her fighting it, but I have to convince her to let me in.

I pull out, flip her over, and slide back in. I lean in as I thrust, slower now. She whimpers, and I know she wants it harder.

"Use your words," I whisper as I nip at her ear. Her legs start to quiver around me. "You close, V? You want to cum all over me?"

"God, yes, Carter."

"Ask me nicely." I give her a hard thrust, and then stay buried as deep as I can go as I wait for her to give me what I want. She stays quiet, wiggling her hips to beg me to move. "That sassy mouth doesn't have much to say when you're stuffed full of my cock, does it?" Another thrust. "Ask for it."

"Please," she begs, and I wish I had the self-control to ask her for more, but I don't. If I hold off any more I'll bust straight through this condom.

I plow into her with everything I have, wrapping my arms around her shoulders to pull her into my chest.

She screams my name so loud I feel a ringing in my ears, but I don't let up until I feel her squeeze my cock so tight it feels like her pussy is pulling my soul from my chest.

I release deep inside her, the condom catching what feels like a nonstop cascade of cum flowing out of me. I grunt into her ear as I slowly grind us both through the aftershocks of our release.

After what feels like forever, I lift myself away from her to look at her face. Her red cheeks and messy hair belong to me right now. I feel myself committing this moment to memory, but hiding the adoration in my eyes.

I don't want her to always be so ready to run.

She doesn't say anything to me, simply lets out a string of deep, slow breaths as she stares right back at me. She doesn't have to say anything though.

I pull out, both of us shaking at the leftover sensitivity. I push off the couch and head straight for the bathroom, disposing of the condom before falling into my bed, balls empty and heart full.

About a minute later, she joins me in the bedroom and helps herself to the bed, spreading out and leaving me with only the very edge. We lie there in silence for a while, letting the fan cool us off.

My room smells like her. Like me. Like sex and something else that feels suspiciously like the 'L' word. But I can't do that to myself. Not yet.

She flips over to her side and tucks her cheek into the crook of my shoulder and chest, tracing lazy shapes in the hollow of my throat and around my Adam's apple. I hold her close, my arm resting comfortably on her hip as if I don't know she's planning how to make her exit without ruining the intimacy of the moment.

The longer we linger in the silence, the more I think. The more I want to say.

"Do you feel it?" I ask.

She doesn't answer, but she lifts her head and begins looking around the room. "Feel what?"

I turn my head to meet her eyes. "This."

She shifts slightly away from me. Just a hair, but the distance might as well be miles. "Carter...please don't."

"I'm not trying to. I'm not. But you can't deny it, can you? We promised we'd be honest."

"Maybe we should practice keeping more thoughts to ourselves," she says, and I think she meant it softly, but it almost snaps out of her like she's already exhausted by the conversation. "I've told you a hundred times this isn't going anywhere."

"But it is. You know it and I know it."

"So let's say I do. Hypothetically. I already told you this will never be serious, so why do you bother bringing it up?"

She says it so coldly, so firmly. Like it's been rehearsed. A speech she's practiced just for the poor guy who can't let her go.

I take a deep breath. "Can I at least know why, V? Please...maybe it would be easier if I understood where you're coming from."

She sits up, but pulls the blankets up to cover her chest. Not running, but it looks like she's getting ready to tell me a horror story.

"I'm broken," she says.

I sit up too, relaxing back on my elbows. "Is that what this is about? A bad heartbreak?"

She shakes her head. "I don't mean heartbroken. I mean really broken. Physically." She goes still and looks down slightly, gathering strength for whatever it is she's trying to tell me. "I lost my virginity when I was fifteen to a senior at my high school. You know...the whole young and in love thing. We didn't use protection and after a few weeks, my period was two days late and I started panicking about possibly being pregnant. I was so scared of ruining both of our lives, and stupidly, I was afraid of him leaving me if he found out. I was afraid my parents would disown me. I didn't know what to do...so I..." She takes a deep breath. "I took my dad's old truck and told him I was going out to the corner store for some soda. But instead of going to the store I—I hit the gas and rammed head-on into a tree hoping that I'd do enough damage to miscarry if I was pregnant."

"Jesus, V," I breathe.

"I know...it was stupid. I was unconscious, but when I finally woke up in the hospital, everything got so much worse."

In my mind, I'm wondering how.

Another deep breath leaves her mouth. "It turns out I did so much internal damage that I had to have a complete hysterectomy at fifteen. They removed my uterus and I completely lost my ability to ever carry children. And the worst part? I was never pregnant to begin with. So I almost killed myself and ruined my future family over nothing."

She looks down in shame, and then with red-rimmed eyes, she gives me an unconvincing smile. "Not exactly first-date material, huh?"

I don't know what to say. Mostly, I feel sorry for that girl that was so scared of a baby that she would go to those lengths to eliminate a possibility she wasn't even sure about. I don't want her to feel exposed, and I'm not sure I want to go back to asking what all this has to do with *us*, so I stay silent.

As if she didn't just pour her heart out to me, she says, "Anyway, I've made peace with it. But guys? Men? It's usually a dealbreaker, especially since we're still technically young. I tell them, and they're nice about it, but the relationship doesn't last long after. Most guys want kids eventually, even if they say they don't when they're young. I get it, but it gets exhausting, so I just do everyone a favor and promise not to get attached right from the beginning."

"You've given up on relationships entirely because of a mistake you made when you were fifteen?" I ask.

"No," she says back, cool as a cucumber. "I just think it's only fair to be upfront about my intentions."

"That's ridiculous," I say.

She gives me a look. "Is it?"

"Yes. You're intelligent, funny, painfully beautiful, and stubborn as hell. If some guy walked away from all of that, that's on him. Not you."

"You don't get it, Carter. It's not fair to ask a man to give up that joy for me."

"Who says a man can't be just as happy with you? Only you. Not to mention there are so many other ways to have kids. Adoption. Fostering. Hell, having a pet. You still deserve to love and be loved for exactly who you are, regardless of your lack of a uterus."

Her expression softens for a second—but only a second.

"Do you want kids?" she asks, like its a test.

"Don't turn this around on me," I warn. "Fuck what I want. This conversation is about you. And V, I'm telling you that I want you, exactly how you are. I wouldn't walk away because of something you can't control."

She doesn't say anything for a while, she simply lies back down and stares at my ceiling. "I don't want to talk about it anymore."

"Okay," I whisper. I mean it. As much as I want to get it through her stubborn little noggin that she's not any less of a person to me because of a trauma she went through years ago, I don't want to push her too hard. Instead, I trace the lines of her face. "How about a shower?" I ask.

She glances over to me, brow raised. "You kicking me out already?"

I grin. "Nah. Just figured I'd cook something while you rinse off. Unless you'd rather sit here marinating in our sins."

She laughs, which is the best sound I've heard all night. "Fine. But I swear, if you're just trying to check out my ass again!"

"No promises," I call over my shoulder as I grab her a fresh towel from my closet.

While she showers, I scoop up her clothes from the floor and toss them into the washer. I turn it on a quick cycle before digging around in my drawer for a clean shirt she can borrow until her clothes are clean.

The fridge is depressing. Two beers, one slightly brown apple, and half a pizza that may or may not be from last Tuesday.

I choose the pizza and beers. *Gourmet, right?*

When she emerges from the bathroom with damp hair clinging to her neck and my shirt around her thighs, it feels so...right. My brain short-circuits, because this is all I could ask for in this moment, and I've got it.

She plops onto the couch and manspreads, revealing her panty-less pussy. My dick stirs, but I ignore it. "Where's my feast?"

I hand her a slice of cold pizza on a one-dollar plate I got from Wal-Mart. In an imitation Italian accent, I say, "It's'a family recipe from mi Nona."

She giggles and takes it without hesitation, taking a big bite. "Perfection."

We end up on the couch, curled under a blanket, watching old cartoons that don't require anything but a low-functioning brain and a few snacks. Her head rests on my shoulder. Her feet are tucked under my thigh.

This is the kind of quiet people dream of. The kind of quiet that doesn't need filling.

"You know," I say after a while, "I meant what I said earlier."

"About what?"

"About how I'd be happy to have you just as you are."

She doesn't respond. But she doesn't pull away either. She just reaches for my hand and holds it like she's testing the waters of something more.

And that? That is enough. *She* is enough.

We watch the screen until our vision goes blurry and our bodies fall limp with sleep. She curls up into my side like a puzzle piece, arm wrapped around my waist and head tucked under my chin.

I don't dare move, not even to move us to the bedroom. I just listen to her breathe, and I appreciate this moment that she's giving me. It's obvious now why she's always tried to be so distant, and I don't want to pretend like this isn't a huge step for her.

The ache in my chest tells me this is never going to be casual again, and I can only hope that she can learn that 'serious' with me will never be scary.

Serious with me means she'll never be alone or unloved again.

Chapter 15 | Venus

Sunlight slides through the blinds in diffused stripes, landing across Carter, casting a pretty glow over his stupidly perfect blond hair.

We're still exactly where we were last night, curled up on the couch and wrapped around each other like we were afraid we'd float away if we let each other go. It's warm and quiet, and for a moment, I allow myself to pretend this perfect little moment will last forever.

Carter's phone alarm begins ringing, and he lifts his head with a groggy grunt before shutting it off. He rubs his palm over his face. "We gotta get up," he mumbles, before sweeping a loose strand of my hair from my face as if it's the most natural thing for him.

I groan and bury my head in his chest. "Already?" I ask, as if I don't already know the answer.

"I've got a shift in a few hours," he says.

I groan again. "Yeah, me too." I sit up and stretch slowly, sore in the best ways and well-rested.

Carter rests his hand on my bare thigh as I pull the elastic out of my hair and readjust my ponytail. "I'll take you home to get ready. Coffee run on the way?" he asks.

"I'm fiending for an egg and cheese bagel sandwich."

Carter chuckles. "We can stop for bagels too."

I smile triumphantly, a new energy in my veins at the prospect of breakfast in my future.

Ten minutes later, we're in his truck with the windows cracked and soft country floating through the speakers. The streets are just beginning to wake up, and there's a biting chill in the air from the turn of the seasons. I rest my forehead against the window and watch the streets pass by as Carter aimlessly drums his fingers on the steering wheel.

We stop at the same cafe all of Terracotta, Georgia gathers at every morning. It's buzzing with every working-age person waiting for their morning fix, and we're no different. We place our order at the drive-through window. Black coffee for him, iced coffee for me. The bagel I've been waiting for is just as delicious as I had hoped it would be, and Carter sneaks a bite while I sip my coffee. An easy silence sits between us like it belongs there, like it knows we don't mind it.

He glances over and in between chews, asks, "You good?"

"Always," I say, still sipping my coffee. "Just a little tired. We were up pretty late."

A smirk finds its way to his lips. "It was worth it though, right?"

Finally, I look over at him and give him a smile that reaches my eyes, saying to him what I know I won't.

When we get to my apartment complex and he drops me off outside my building, Callie is waiting outside, sitting on the trunk of her Honda waiting for me with a proud smile on her face. She gives Carter a friendly wave.

I meet Carter's eyes and give him a small smile. "Thanks for the bagel, and the orgasms. Text me later?"

"If you're good," he says, like he knows that's not gonna happen.

I smirk. "Me? Good? Always," I say, before hopping out of the truck and running into my apartment to change.

The hospital is chaos, as per usual. Labor and delivery is never quiet. Between check-ins, screaming through contractions, new babies, and emergency c-sections, Callie and I barely have time to breathe, or pee.

God, I have to pee.

By the early afternoon, the morning coffee has completely worn off and I'm running on fumes. With only a few minutes to myself, I duck into a supply closet to 'grab an extra blanket for a new mom' to finally let out a real exhale.

It smells like baby powder and alcohol in here, and it about perfectly sums up the shift. I reach into the shelves, rummaging around for nothing to keep myself looking busy when the door cracks just a second after it closes behind me.

I expect it to be another nurse looking for supplies, but instead, a hand wraps around my mouth and another pulls me backward into a hard body.

"Shhhh."

"Carter!" I gasp, turning around to face him. We're practically in each other's clothes with how tight this closet is. "What are you doing here?"

His hand touches my stomach and then trails downward, sliding right under the waistband of my scrubs like he pays rent in there.

I freeze, hesitating at the thought of someone walking in, but then his fingers touch me, and I melt. Instantly. All inhibitions gone.

His mouth brushes my ear. "Brought someone into the ER. Couldn't stop thinking about you so I slipped away to come find you. Don't worry, I'll make it quick. But I needed this. I needed you."

My brain tries to file a complaint, form an objection, but my body shuts it down.

I grab the collar of his shirt and yank him closer, stumbling back and hitting the shelves behind me with a soft *thunk*. Boxes rattle above me and giant pads rain unsexily around us, but I don't care.

His fingers curl inside me as soon as they slip in, pulling a gasp from my throat.

"Be *quiet*," he murmurs, grinning like the absolute menace he is, knowing he's wrecking absolute havoc on my body. "Be *good*."

As he begins to pump his fingers inside me, I reach into his pants and squeeze his length. He groans quietly into my ear and we both decide in the same moment that we want to make the other break. He adds his thumb to rub circles on my clit while I focus my attention on his head, spreading his precum around to make the movements easier.

I bite my lip to keep a moan from slipping out, but he's using the curve of my neck as his salvation to keep quiet. I bet he's leaving a mark, but that's an issue I'll have to deal with later.

All I care about right now is the way his fingers are touching me in the most delicious way. He's fulfilling a craving I didn't even realize I was having until now.

It's rushed, reckless, and a mess of hands and heat and shared desperation. I bite down on the inside of my cheek to keep from gasping. He groans quietly into the side of my throat and I feel it in my spine. The whole damn supply closet blurs until there's nothing left except him and me and the pulse in my cooch.

And as soon as we're done dressing, he backs away like nothing happened. He adjusts his pants, shoots me a wink, and leaves.

Just leaves.

I stand pressed against a shelf of newborn diapers, trying to remember how to do my job. My scrubs are rumpled and my heart continues to race as I straighten them out. I smooth down my hair before randomly grabbing a few supplies and stepping back into the hallway just like he did.

Like nothing happened. Like he didn't just completely wreck me.

As soon as I leave the closet, the world returns to normal. Nurses share updates, monitors are beeping, supervisors make small talk. Callie offers me half of her granola bar.

I find a random room and deliver the blanket to the new mother, and she thanks me for being so thoughtful and thinking of her. I smile with masterful deception, accepting her appreciation as if my actions truly were altruistic.

The next room over, I watch as an overly-cautious couple changes their new baby's diaper, asking if they're doing it right every five seconds. Then I move on. Chart. Answer phones. Check on mothers. Pretend my skin isn't on fire and Carter isn't on my mind.

Pretend like I can't hear him whispering in my ear.

Hours later, at the very end of my shift, I finally take a seat at the nurse's station. I'm exhausted, but somehow dying for attention from a certain firefighter.

My phone buzzes in my pocket.

Speak of the devil.

Carter: Worth it?

I stare at his name for a second, then answer.

Me: Maybe.

Me: I think we should try it again, just to be sure.

Chapter 16 | Venus

The next time I see Carter, we're with the whole crew. Callie, Jackson, Trevor, and a mixture of hospital staff and firefighters. We're loud, but that's just because we know how to have a good time. We crowd into the parking lot of an old bowling alley on the edge of town.

Whoever decided that a glitchy, sticky arcade filled with neon signs should get stuck to a bowling alley with pins that look like they've been scavenged from a dumpster?

Genius.

Sure, maybe the bathrooms are gross enough to make you hold your bladder the whole night and maybe there's a rat the size of a baby lingering somewhere in the kitchen, but this is the kind of place where real memories are made.

I've traded in my crop tops and denim shorts for leggings and a sweater. Still got my boots, though.

Mostly to protect my feet from whatever diseases are multiplying in the old carpet. This place has scarier floors than the hospital.

Carter and I slide in behind everyone else, not in any rush. We've got all night. Three whole days of no shifts, no commitments, and I couldn't be more excited about it.

Carter and I have been texting a ton since he jumped me in the supply closet at work, and I find myself missing him when he's busy.

Missing him a lot.

Silence without him is so uncomfortable. It's got this tension to it that I'm not sure I like. But as soon as I saw him across the parking lot, stepping out of his old truck and meeting my eyes, I felt...okay. Normal. At peace.

Inside the arcade, the group naturally splits into smaller groups. Some go to the bar. Some go to grab shoes and a bowling lane. Others exchange their loose bills for arcade tokens.

Naturally, the boys insist they can dominate anyone at skee-ball. Men seem to think that about anything that requires low brain power, zero strategy, and a big ego.

They're gonna learn today.

I slide a few tokens into the machine, tie up my hair, and grab a ball. I lightly toss it into the air in challenge. "Y'all ready to get humbled?"

Callie gives me a knowing smirk. Trevor rolls his eyes like I've personally insulted every ounce of masculinity in his steroid-pumped muscles. Jackson snickers like he thinks my bravery's cute.

Carter? He looks ready for war. "Game on," he taunts.

"Show me what you've got, big man."

And he does. He makes some good shots in the beginning, but sinks his last four. Jackson does even worse.

Trevor? He doesn't even score 5,000 points.

He shrugs as if it's not bothering him. "It's just skee-ball. Who cares?"

I make a crying face and pretend to rub my eyes, mocking him. "Awww, is the little baby gonna cry because he's gonna lose to a girl?"

"Big words coming from someone who hasn't even played yet," Carter interjects, defending his friend's honor.

I turn around, line up my shot, and sink my first ball into the 50,000 point slot at the top. Clean.

Carter looks at me, mouth wide in disbelief. "What the hell?"

I stick my tongue out. "What was that about big words?" I ask, before sinking yet another shot. This time in the 10,000 point hole.

Eight balls later, and I've beaten the high score in the arcade, triumphantly typing 'Venus' into the screen. I don't even have to gloat, the boys know their place. When I turn around from the high-score screen, Carter is leaning against the wall behind me. He's got this quiet, focused look on his face. Something like yearning. Like he's been studying me and not the scoreboard.

Eventually, the group gets smaller. More intimate. Trevor and Jackson head straight for the snack bar. Callie left with a wink and is flirting with one of the other firefighters, leaving Carter and I alone.

He knows what I want. I've been throwing him sultry glances and *accidental* touches all night. I don't say anything. I simply turn my back to him and head in the direction of the restrooms and storage closets that hide in the very back corner of the arcade.

I know he'll follow. I can feel it in his stare. In his energy.

I slip into the storage closet and he slips in right behind me. The old wooden door shuts away the rest of the world, leaving us in the dark.

"This looks familiar," he says with a knowing glint in his eyes.

I meet his stare and hoist myself up onto an old shelf. He clicks on the overhead light, a single bulb above our heads. It hums as if it's a giant alarm telling everyone how much sexual tension is concealed behind the door.

The room smells like lemon-scented floor cleaner, but the air was thick with something more than just that chemical smell. It was desire. Heat. Want.

Maybe even something I'm too afraid to admit.

From his place at the door, Carter prowls toward me like a predator calculating his attack. His eyes trace up and down my body like he's never seen it before. The fabric at the front of his pants is taut from the strain behind them.

When he positions himself in front of me, he drops to his knees with a soft thud. His eyes stare into my soul, sharklike with the ache to touch me–to taste me.

I forget how to breathe as he pulls my leggings down my legs with slow, calculated precision. He doesn't even bother taking them all the way off. He gets them about halfway down my calves and then hoists my legs over his shoulders.

He takes a deep breath as he stares at my sex, and the warmth from his mouth sends shivers up my spine. My fingers wrap around the edge of the shelf, and when that's not enough, I wrap them in his hair.

When his tongue delves into me, I throw my head back and sigh, and then he does that thing with his tongue he knows I like. The one where he circles my clit with just enough pressure to make me–

"Ah, Carter," I moan.

"We're just getting started, V. Someone's worked up."

I let out half a laugh before I suck in a sharp breath at the feeling of him licking up and down my center. I try not to fall apart completely as he takes his time. He works me over like it's his favorite thing to do. Like with everything in his life, he's laser focused. Methodical and maybe just a little bit cruel because he knows I like that.

He knows exactly what he's doing, pushing me so close to the edge only to pull back and start over again. He edges me until I'm nearly in tears, crying his name and begging for him to fuck me like only he can.

Just when I think he's about to give me what I want, he pulls back and moves my legs from off his shoulders.

"Carter!" I groan out, horny and frustrated and dripping wet.

His mouth is glistening, and his eyes are hot enough to set me on fire.

Vulcan, indeed.

"If you want more," he says, low and smug as he licks his lips, "you'll have to wait."

My mouth falls open. "That is messed up."

"You'll live," he says with a grin.

"Next time you want me to suck your dick, I'll remember this."

He winks at me. "Looking forward to it."

Then he backs out of the room and steps into the men's bathroom to wash off his face, leaving me standing there in a cupboard and wetter than the mop.

It takes me a few minutes to remember how to use my legs for anything other than spreading them for a firefighter with a skillful tongue. When I emerge, Carter is leaning against the wall, arms and legs crossed. The picture of smug nonchalance.

"You look cute when you're blushing," he teases.

"You'd look cute with my foot three feet up your ass."

"Kinky."

I roll my eyes and we join the rest of the crew again. If anyone knows about how we just defiled that closet, they say nothing.

Later in the night, long after everyone should be in bed, including me, I show up at Carter's door.

No heads up. No text. I just...show up. I don't even know why I do, and I don't remember the drive here. I haven't even changed or showered yet, too preoccupied with thoughts of him.

He opens the door, looking half surprised and half like he's expecting a confession.

I don't give him one. Instead, I step into his apartment with no rush, no teasing, no tension.

Just him and I and the space between our bodies slowly fading away. I think a part of me knows this isn't casual anymore, but I can't allow that. I don't want it and he knows it.

I need to let this all go before I start falling harder, but I can't. I don't want to.

I can't be with him. He knows it, even if he doesn't see me in the same broken way that I do.

But I also feel sick at the thought of never seeing him again after this is all over. I can't see us just being...friends after all of this.

But all of those thoughts fade away when he kisses me like he's been waiting to do it all night. It's filled with everything he shouldn't say to me, so he has to show me instead.

I let him undress me piece by piece, and let his hands learn every inch of me like it matters how well he knows it. Like I'm not meant to be just another body in the dark.

When we land on the bed, he doesn't fuck me frantically. He doesn't fight me for control. He doesn't try to impress me.

It's just us. Him and I, letting ourselves fit together like the puzzle pieces he so desperately wants us to be.

After we finish, I lie with my head against his chest, listening to his steady heartbeat in the heavy but warm silence. I trace shapes on his chest like I've done a dozen times before.

"So are you always that bad at skee-ball?" I ask quietly.

He laughs, low and gravely. "Maybe I just like letting you win."

I smile against his bare skin. "Sure you do."

He doesn't reply, and he doesn't have to. The world keeps spinning, but right here, in this room, wrapped up in this man who so clearly adores me, I feel like things might be okay.

And that scares me more than anything.

Chapter 17 | Vulcan

I'm halfway through a turkey sandwich and the fourth quarter of a Falcons game when the call comes through.

Terracotta Engine One respond. We've got a report of smoke from building B of the Briarview Apartments. No visible flames reported. Neighbors can hear a fire alarm from Unit 23.

I freeze.

Briarview.

That's Venus' apartment complex. If this town wasn't so small, I don't think I'd recognize the name. But it's hers, so I do. The last bite of my sandwich turns to ash in my mouth as I stand, grab my gear, and head down to the engine, already roaring and ready to go.

I sneak a call to Venus on my cellphone, but she doesn't answer, and I feel my hands begin to grow sweaty with panic.

Trevor shouts from the bay, "Let me guess. That's the building with the Nurse Hottie you keep pretending you don't still think about? Don't sweat it man, this building's fire alarms are shit. It's probably just a false."

Suddenly, I'm not sure I remember her apartment number correctly. Is she in Unit 23B? Or is it 32B? Or is it not even in building B at all? I can't think straight, an uncomfortable worry racing through my veins.

Leroy rumbles down the road ten minutes later, sirens quiet this time, just lights spinning red across windows and windshields. The call doesn't sound urgent, but my pulse doesn't seem to care. It's beating like we've pulled a child out of a burning hallway.

When we pull up to the apartment complex, there's no smoke. No crowd. Just one old woman standing on the sidewalk in slippers, clutching a cat like a purse.

I hop out first and approach the leasing office rep who flagged us down. "Which unit?"

"Top floor. 23B. Neighbor called in a loud alarm."

"Anyone inside?"

"Don't know. No one's answering."

I nod. Try not to run.

I hit the stairwell with Jackson and Trevor behind me. The hallway reeks of cheap air freshener and laundry soap. The alarm's going off, high-pitched and shrill, like a metal scream jammed into my brain. We bang on the door.

"Fire department! Anyone inside?"

Nothing.

Another knock, louder this time. Trevor checks the door.

"It's locked."

I'm already stepping back. "Forcing entry."

"Maybe we should—"

I ignore the protest and don't even care about the likelihood of getting written up for forcing entry without permission, but I don't care.

One solid kick. Then two. The door bursts open with a crack that echoes down the hall.

And then, she's there, standing in the middle of her kitchen. Barefoot. Hair piled on her head in a messy bun. Stubborn mascara that didn't come off in the shower under her eyes.

She's wearing a t-shirt that I instantly recognize as one I've been searching for in my apartment for three days.

She's holding a frying pan in one hand and a towel in the other, and she's got headphones blaring over her ears. Her smoke alarm is screaming overhead.

And she has the nerve to look at me like *I'm* the emergency.

"What the hell, Carter?" she yells over the beeping, setting down the pan and pulling the headphones off her head. "Are you kicking down my door now?"

My heart stumbles and restarts. "You weren't answering."

"Because I was fanning smoke out the window!" she snaps. "I burned a grilled cheese!"

Jackson enters behind me, confused. "So... not a fire?"

"No," she says, dramatically wiping her forehead. "Just a tragic culinary misstep. I was trying to do something normal for once. Bad idea, apparently."

Trevor peeks in. "Smells like regret."

"Smells like cheddar," Jackson mutters.

I'm still staring at her. Still winded. "You're okay?"

She freezes at the tone of my voice.

The sarcasm slips. The fight goes out of her shoulders. "Yeah," she says quietly. "I'm fine."

The alarm keeps shrieking.

I step forward, climb onto a chair, and disable it with a practiced flick of the wrist. Silence crashes into the apartment like a wave.

"Thanks," she murmurs.

"Next time, *answer the damn door*," I say, trying to sound like I'm not still shaking.

She folds her arms. "Didn't expect the entire station to show up."

Trevor grins. "Well, *someone* panicked. Practically leapt out of the truck and tackled your neighbor like a linebacker on the way up the stairs."

I shoot him a look. "Get back downstairs. Secure the perimeter."

"There's no perimeter," Jackson protests.

"Make one."

Trevor gives me a mocking look and salutes me. "Yes, Lieutenant."

They leave, smirking.

I'm alone with her now. And now that the adrenaline's fading, something else starts creeping in.

I look around her apartment. It's small, clean, but cluttered in a human way, like there's signs of a busy life that takes refuge here after a long day. A soft throw blanket sits half-tangled on the couch. A pair of clean scrubs hanging on a Command hook on the bedroom door. A dog-eared paperback on the counter, pages wavy and discolored from a coffee stain.

"You know, if you wanted to see me that bad, you could have just said so. Kicking down my door was a little dramatic."

"I tried calling. You didn't answer. I thought you were in danger."

"I was. Burnt cheese is a three-alarm emergency, clearly." She looks toward the door and scowls slightly. "You're paying for the repair."

I step closer, ignoring her. "Don't scare me like that again, okay? I'm sorry about your door, but there was an alarm and no answer. I was just doing my job."

She gives me a half-smile. "I know. Thank you, Carter. But I'm fine. Really. My music was too loud, I just didn't hear the alarm."

I look at her for a long time, memorizing every strand of that curly blonde hair piled high on her head. Remembering how soft her skin feels under my fingertips.

Remembering that pain in my stomach every time we say goodbye after a night together.

Right now, standing here in her apartment with the false fire and the real tension between us, I realize something I wasn't exactly sure of before, but I'm definitely sure of now.

I love her.

Not just that sickly-sweet puppy love that usually creeps up between two friends, but strong, confident love. The kind of love that makes you dread the goodbyes but count down the seconds to the hellos. The kind of love where I look at her and the first word that comes to mind is: *home*.

I love her.

"You okay?" I ask again, just to check.

She looks at me for a long second. "Yeah. Fine."

I nod to the charred remains of her sandwich. "Grilled cheese is DOA though. I'll pass on the message to the next of kin."

"Isn't it pathetic that I'm quickly approaching thirty and can't cook a grilled cheese without summoning the entire fire department?"

I shrug and give her a chuckle. "You might be terrible at grilled cheese, but I'm decent at pasta. I'll show you tonight. For dinner."

"You just kicked down my door and now you want to play house?" she teases. Then, she gives me a smug expression. "Well, I guess I'll be needing somewhere to stay while my door gets repaired."

I give her a smile back. "I'll make a reservation for you at the Westwood Bed & Breakfast." I look around. "What about Callie?"

"She's conveniently out of town for the next two days for her little brother's college graduation. So we'll just need one bed, please."

"Alright, but you'll have to share the space with the owner. I hear he's *smokin'* hot."

She flicks the kitchen towel at me, making a snapping sound to ward me out the door.

"Bye, Carter!"

Chapter 18 | Vulcan

My apartment smells like bold, citrusy shampoo. It smells like *her*.

And I fucking love it.

I know she only agreed to sleep here for a few nights while her apartment door gets repaired, but the way I felt when I woke up this morning, knowing she was here, knowing she would stay?

It's magical. Surreal. I never want it to end.

She's sitting at my tiny round table near the kitchen, sipping on a Redbull. The sunlight filters through the blinds and curtains, casting the floor and her bare shoulders in pretty golden lines.

This is the kind of morning peace that you never want to end.

"Want some pancakes?" I ask, already reaching for the mix in the pantry. She hums and nods back. I flip on the TV to watch the morning news, and she raises her head from the daily crossword puzzle on her phone to watch the coverage.

Breaking News! The infamous East Coast billionaire Christian Reeves and his wife Elena were found shot to death in their home this morning, along with both of Mrs. Reeves' parents.

Preliminary police reports believe this to be the result of a triple-murder suicide, but details are unclear on which individual is responsible. The MCPD has been keeping this case very tightly guarded while they investigate.

The Reeves' recently adopted a child, who we can confirm was found safe in the home by the family's private chef, who has not agreed to any interviews and refuses to comment on what he saw inside the home.

The fate of the Reeves Empire remains unknown, and stock prices have plummeted due to investor uncertainty—

"Jesus. I've seen some things, but I can't even imagine," I say, mindlessly flipping the golden brown pancakes onto a plate and coating them with syrup.

That's the thing about working in a job like firefighting or nursing...you sorta grow numb to that kind of violence or tragedy after a while. You get a few that stick with you, but otherwise you just learn to say *'that's terrible'* and continue eating breakfast.

It's mostly just background noise for me this time, but V seems more upset the longer she watches the footage of the red, white and blue lights surrounding that mansion. She seems to enter another dimension, her eyes absorbing the pictures on the screen but her mind racing a million miles a minute. I don't interrupt her, just watch her face twist and turn with whatever emotions she's trying to work through.

"That poor baby wakes up and her whole world is just...gone," she murmurs, her pancakes now cold and untouched.

I don't answer. What am I supposed to say? Of course I can't imagine it. I've pulled kids out of cars, dragged them through smoke, held the hands of ones who tearfully waited for parents who will never come back, but my life—my world—always kept turning. How is a kid that young even supposed to understand what's happening, let alone know how to process the grief that takes up residence in their lives uninvited?

Venus keeps watching the screen. "This is just another reason I won't commit," she says. She lets it out so easily, like there's not a man who adores her sitting across the table right now. "When I die, I hope no one mourns me."

That feels like a dagger in my chest. She hates a part of herself she lost so long ago. She hates it so much that she almost wishes for loneliness. Begs for it.

I wish there was something I could say to change her mind, but even if I could, now isn't the right time. She wouldn't respond well to words, and I hate the way her shoulders sag as she tries to convince herself she's really unworthy of love—of even being grieved.

Without thinking, I lean over and kiss her temple. Soft. Quick. Not even romantic. Not anything other than a gesture of comfort.

She flinches like I've just slapped her, and I know in that very instant, that I've made a mistake.

She stills, and her body turns toward me. Not in a soft way or an inviting way, but like I've stumbled into a tripwire and alerted her to danger.

She says nothing, just stands up and walks to my room. When she hears my chair scrape across the floor she waves at me, still facing away.

"Just give me a second," she says, completely void of any emotion—not even anger or panic. Just...nothing.

"I'm sorry...I was just—"

"I know. I know you didn't mean anything by it." She finally turns to face me and crosses her arms over her chest, visibly uncomfortable. "But the problem is that you did. You wanted to. You needed to. We can't...we can't keep doing this. This was always supposed to be just sex, remember?"

"It's never been just sex to me, and I think you know that. I wasn't trying to cross a line, but I care about you, V. Why won't you let me?"

"What makes you think I want or need you to care about me? You don't even know my name."

"Fuck. Seriously? I get that I stepped over the line, but you have no right to choose who I do and don't care about."

She completely ignores me and motions between us with her hands. "This thing between us, whatever we've been doing, needs to go back to casual. I've always been honest about what I've wanted out of this and I let you get too close and I'm sorry. But this" she motions between us again, "is not happening. It's never going to happen."

I stand there, my chest aching with hurt. I never expected her to be so...cruel. I don't even know what to say anymore. I rub my face, and she disappears into my room and emerges a few minutes later with her bag.

"I forgot I promised Callie I'd do some stuff with her today. I should go."

She doesn't even have the courage to look at me when she walks out, and I don't bother trying to stop her.

I simply say, "be safe" under my breath, and then she's gone.

My apartment has never felt so hollow. Pancakes untouched. The TV is still playing news coverage, but I don't hear it anymore.

Maybe I shouldn't have kissed her. Maybe comforting her wasn't my job. Maybe a part of me did want to cross a line just to see how she would react.

But this isn't even about romance or our future. It's watching someone I care about shoulder a burden on her shoulders I'm willing to share with her.

I can only hope that this distance she's put between us is temporary, because I don't want to imagine my world without her in it.

Chapter 19 | Venus

The fluorescent lights in the labor and delivery ward buzz overhead like always. Too bright, too loud, and too sterile. I step off the elevator and into the usual chaos. Soft beeping monitors. A nurse laughing down the hall. Someone crying behind a closed curtain. All of it familiar, all of it steady.

I pull my badge over my scrubs and check the clock: 7 AM. Right on time. Unfortunately.

My phone buzzes in my pocket. I don't need to look to know who it is. There's only one person it could be and it's the same person I don't want to hear from this morning, the rest of the day, or maybe even the rest of forever.

Carter: I'm really sorry about earlier. I didn't mean to overstep. Hope work goes okay today.

I stare at the message for a beat too long, then lock my phone and shove it back into my pocket without responding.

It isn't that I'm mad.

Okay—maybe I'm a little mad.

But mostly, I don't know what there is to say. I've been crystal clear from the beginning. No expectations. No mess. Just sex when there's time in our busy lives. Just something that doesn't ask too much of me and has even fewer expectations.

Lately though, everything between us has started to shift. Lines are more blurry, gestures are more meaningful, and things started getting a little too fluffy to be purely casual.

That kiss on the forehead was too much. Too close for comfort. Too natural for him to just do without even thinking.

I roll my shoulders back and walk to the nurses' station, already scanning the board—two scheduled inductions, an emergency C-section pending, and a first-time mom having a slow panic attack in triage. *Perfect.* A full slate.

Work is the only place where everything makes sense right now. Where I'm in control and no one tries to make me feel more than I want to.

Somehow, between the running back and forth and the changing into a fresh pair of scrubs because a newborn peed all over me, Callie catches me.

"You okay?" she asks, eying me over like she's checking for injuries.

"Yeah?" I say, losing myself in a chart. She gives me an unconvinced look, but moves on. If she knows one thing about me, it's not to push. She knows I'll talk about things when I'm ready to, and not a second sooner.

By noon, I've helped deliver twins and scrubbed in on a C-section. After that, I guide a woman through a Pitocin contraction that makes her scream like she's being split in half. There's no room for thinking about firefighters on this shift, which is exactly what I needed.

Callie and I meet after our shift at the hotel room she's been staying at after the fire alarm in our apartment building. There was no way I was going back to Carter's, but I know that her letting me crash here comes with a steep payment of spilling the beans.

"You look like shit," Callie says, stepping out of the steamy bathroom with a towel on top of her head.

"You look like you need a knuckle sandwich."

She snorts. "Are you five?"

I roll my eyes. "Shut up and get to it already."

She smiles, jumps on the bed, and pulls a blanket on top of her legs like she's getting ready for story time. "I want to know everything."

I sigh. "It's Carter."

She looks at me like I've just insulted her. "Duh. No one else would have you moping around all day like this. What happened?"

"He caught feelings. Strong ones, even though I told him from the beginning and about a dozen times after that I don't want serious. The last time I saw him...he kissed me on the forehead."

Callie gives me a look of complete disbelief. "You're shitting your pants over a kiss?"

"It's not just the kiss!" I say defensively. "It was what was behind the kiss. I felt it. We were watching a sad news story that was really getting to me and—"

"And...he comforted you in a totally normal way?"

"Kissing your bootycall on the forehead is not normal. And that's not even the point. The point is, he felt that things were casual enough between us to do it in the first place."

Callie waves her hands to get me to stop talking. "So let me get this straight. You're at his house more than your own apartment. You go out all the time. He brings you coffee and lunch randomly. He bought a loofah for you to keep in his shower, and last week I found *his* shirt in *our* washing machine...but a kiss on the forehead was too casual for you?"

"Yes," I say absolutely, though it does sound incredibly ridiculous when she says it out loud. I rub my temples. "None of that stuff gives him the right to start acting like we have something when I've told him I don't want that."

"V," she says gently. "Don't you think this was kinda inevitable? Anyone with eyes can see how good you two are for each other. It was inevitable someone was going to catch feelings, it just happened to be him because you're emotionally constipated."

I feel something twist in my heart. "I told him my boundaries."

"Uh-huh. And every time you assert them, does he respect it?"

"Yes, but—"

"And what did he do when you told him the kiss made you uncomfortable?"

"He apologized, but—"

Callie snaps to get me to shut up again. "Wake *up*, girl. What else could you want from that man? Space? He's giving it to you right now."

I don't answer.

"You're not in the wrong for being scared. I get it. You have your reasons. But Carter...he's different. I see it, and I know you see it even if you won't admit it to yourself. The guy is crazy about you and he's not going to stop feeling that way. And feeling something back isn't going to kill you, V. It might be scary, and yeah, maybe it doesn't work out in the end. But that doesn't mean it isn't worth trying. You deserve your own happily ever after."

I pull out my phone again, open the messaging app, and stare at the message from this morning.

Carter: I'm really sorry about earlier. I didn't mean to overstep. Hope work goes okay today.

I think about it, long and hard. His message isn't clingy or loaded. It's...thoughtful and careful. He knew he needed to say something, but still gave me the room I needed to work out these confusing feelings.

I still don't reply. Not because I don't want to, but because when I do, I think Carter deserves to know where we stand, and I'm still trying to figure that out myself.

Chapter 20 | Vulcan

I'm halfway through a protein bar and a Monster energy drink. Boots off, hogging the entire bunkroom couch while the low murmur of an old documentary plays in the background. The station is quiet, with the always-lingering smell of coffee, sweat, and soot that never quite leaves no matter how often we mop the floors.

My phone vibrates, and I jolt upright when I see the name on the screen.

Venus: You busy tonight?

Just like that. No emoji. No excited punctuation. An uncomplicated question with a very complicated answer.

Me: Sorry. On shift until tomorrow morning.

Venus: Tomorrow night, then?

I stare at the screen for much longer than needed, just trying to form rational thoughts. I know what she wants. She's made it very clear it's the only thing she's willing to take from me, despite me being so ready to give her everything.

Me: What time?

Venus: 10?

Me: Okay.

I drop my phone into my lap and rub my face with both hands, stretching the skin under my eyes, hoping that when my skin pops back into place it will knock some sense into me.

It doesn't.

A few weeks ago, her texts asking to meet up would have had me cleaning the apartment, giving my face a fresh shave, maybe even stocking the fridge with her favorite snacks. Maybe even shaving my nuts.

Do you know how uncomfortable shaving your nuts is?

Now, though? Her texts just sit uneasy in my gut. Sits heavy on my chest like a weight that's waiting to crush me flat into the ground.

The thing we had before, it worked when it was new. It worked when I didn't care, or at least tried to tell myself I didn't.

Now? It just hurts. Like an inevitable breakup, and we were never together in the first place. Just a dull and constant ache that I can't remedy with ibuprofen.

Venus has always been clear with me. She didn't want strings and she didn't want pressure. She just wanted a good time. For a while, I was happy to give her that, but it's become too obvious that it's no longer enough for me.

I want her laugh to echo off the walls in the morning and her snoring to fill my ears every night. I want her to tell me how her day went in the morning after a shift while she showers and I brush my teeth.

I don't want her to leave after a good night. I want her to stay.

And that's the exact opposite of what she wants.

For a moment, I think about canceling. Just texting her back and making up some sorry excuse for why I can't see her.

But I don't, because the truth is, I'm not ready to let her go, even if every part of me is screaming to just get it over with to protect myself from any more hurt.

I finish my shift. Three false alarms and a tiny trash fire. Nothing that wears me out enough to give her a truthful excuse of *'I'm tired'* to cancel on her. So I drive home, take a long, hot shower, and try to pull myself together enough to try and convince her to stay this time.

I'm still dripping wet, trying to use my towel to remove the conditioner I didn't rinse out well enough from my hair when I hear a knock on my door. I wrap the towel around my hips and walk to the door, peeking through the peephole.

I check the clock hanging above my couch. 9:42. She's early.

My heart jumps as if it doesn't know any better. When I open the door, she's standing there in a hoodie she's stolen from me and a smile brighter than the sun. I wish I could give her that same smile back, but I can't, and she notices.

Her smile falls. "Hey," she says.

"Hey," I reply, trying to keep my voice normal. I find myself leaning against the doorframe, almost blocking her way in. Her eyes sweep over my wet hair and bare chest. "Sorry, you're a little early."

She shrugs. "I was bored."

Yeah. That's the problem. I'm the sucker she runs to when she's bored.

"But I can come back if you need some extra time to get pretty for me," she adds.

"No, you're good. Just give me a sec to get dressed."

She walks past me like she belongs in my apartment, like how I desperately wished she did. I close the door behind her and she drops her bag and tosses off her hoodie. Underneath, that red lace bra from before.

"You don't need clothes," she says, before stripping off her leggings too.

Like the sad, lovesick man that I am, I give her exactly what she wants. No bargaining, no sweet kisses, no anything that would make this mean anything to her.

I get on my knees and pull her panties down her legs. I hook one of her thighs over my shoulder and suck on her clit from my place on the ground. She grinds her hips on my face, spreading her wetness across my lips and chin.

I try to keep eye contact with her, but it's almost like she knows that's what I want, and so she looks everywhere but at me. Like she doesn't want to see what she's done to me.

She doesn't want to see how much I want more than just sex.

Like she can feel my thoughts, she steps away from me, takes my hand, and pulls me to the bedroom. She climbs on the bed, face down, ass up, wiggling her hips and showing me exactly what she wants from me.

But if this is really what she wants, then I want her to see me. So I force her to flip over. Not in a rough way, but in a desperate way. She finally finds the courage to look at me, and only then do I slip inside her. No condom this time.

Just me and her and nothing in between.

And I do mean literally nothing. She's looking at me, but there's nothing there. It's like she's a shell. The walls I've spent so long trying to break through with love, she's rebuilt them.

I snap my hips into hers, no longer interested in prolonging this. This should be a beautiful moment, but instead, it's just two people who couldn't be more opposite in their expectations, pretending everything is okay.

She grabs my shoulders and forces my head into her neck, no longer willing to look at me, and I don't fight it. I simply fuck her like she wants.

Emotionlessly. Passionless.

I seat myself deep inside her when I come, and I'm not even sure I paid attention to if she finished as well.

But this is the kind of inattentiveness she should expect from sex that should mean nothing.

This is what she wants, right? So I shouldn't force myself to feel bad about it.

When we catch our breath still tangled in each other's arms, there's a moment that lasts no more than a millisecond, where she looks like maybe she's considering staying.

But I know better than that.

"It's late. I'm kinda beat from work. You should probably head out soon," I say, though it's really not what I want.

She stiffens. "Oh," she whispers, then untangles herself from me. "Right. Yeah."

A stupid part of my heart convinces me I see a flicker of hurt in her eyes, but I know better than that, too.

She gets dressed in silence, facing away from me to save us both the awkward glances.

I don't want her to leave, but I also don't want my heart to feel like a liability to her.

No dinner. No small talk. No breakfast.

She texts, I answer. We meet, we fuck, we leave.

That's our pattern for a month.

At first, it's a way for me to take back control of this thing we have. I follow the rules, never overstaying my welcome or bombarding her with my feelings. I tell myself that this is better, that I'm saving myself the heartbreak.

But by the fourth or fifth time, it starts wearing down on me, like a grindstone straight to my soul. Every time I see her, it now fills me with dread. I'm cold, robotic, and hollow when I'm around her. Literally a different person than when I'm with my buddies or anyone else.

I'm no longer saving myself the heartbreak, just prolonging it.

Venus is different too. She smiles less. She's quieter. She's less mouthy, which is one of the things I love about her.

But she never bothers to ask why I've suddenly grown detached, and the longer this goes on, the less I think she cares. I won't bother giving her any more of me, and I won't offer her another version of this.

One, because I'm scared she'll say no, and two, because she's always made it so clear to me that it's not what she wants.

This time, when the door closes behind her, I go back to my room and sit on the edge of my bed. I stare at my rumpled sheets that still linger with her scent. My chest feels tight. My throat burns.

This isn't working for me. Not anymore. I'm not willing to keep going like this—with this distance between us.

I miss her laugh and the way she borrows my socks while hers are in my washing machine. The way she hums while she brushes her teeth and steals a handful of black licorice before she leaves.

I miss her. Not the hookup or the distraction. Her.

I get up and walk to the kitchen, filling a glass of water from the tap. I take a small sip and stare at my empty apartment. It feels uncomfortably big and void of life. This has been my home for years, but suddenly, it's missing something.

And I know exactly what it is.

Or rather—who.

The next time she texts me comes just the next day.

Venus: Free tonight?

I don't reply right away, just let it sit there while I stare at the words on the screen.

I want her, I do. Just not like this.

Me: Can we talk first?

She reads the message. Then a typing bubble pops up. Then disappears. Then comes back before disappearing again, before it leaves for good.

No response. The phone is as empty as my apartment.

I wait aimlessly on my couch with a movie on mute in the background. I just want an answer, even if it confirms this is as one-sided as it feels.

She never bothers replying. I tell myself she's just busy...or just forgot to press send. I set my phone down and resist the urge to check it every few seconds. I even ignore the phantom vibrations. Just let it sit there.

On the back of my phone case, there's a holographic sticker of a stegosaurus that she won from the bowling alley. It's a harmless, stupid thing, but it's something else that hurts my chest.

Just another reminder of something I can't have.

I don't know if she'll reply, but even if she doesn't, I need to tell her the truth. Just let her know what's going on with us from my perspective, and hope to God she'll meet me halfway. I want to be seen by her. I want her to choose this. Choose us.

I can't keep carving myself up into little pieces just to keep her more comfortable.

If she's not even willing to hear me out, then I'll have to let her go.

Even if it splits me open.

Chapter 21 | Venus

My gas pump clicks off automatically with a loud *thunk*. I yank the nozzle out and shove it back into its dirty cradle with more force than necessary. I've been a mess these past few days. My head is in another galaxy.

I thought seeing Carter again would fix everything and that things would feel normal again, but I was so wrong. He showed up, puppy dog eyes begging me to tell him everything will be okay. Instead of giving that to him, I gave him my body instead.

And I could tell by the end of it that it wasn't enough for him. The way he looked at me, so defeated but hopeful, made me want to crawl out of my own skin.

I should have seen this coming. Scratch that—I did see this coming. The jokes softened. The silences became more comfortable. The trauma-dumping happened. The way he began to touch me suddenly felt different. He was no longer just undressing me, but aching to understand me.

And I let him. I didn't stop him. Not even once. Because I stupidly told myself it was harmless. I told myself he knew what he got into and he wasn't really falling.

But he did, and I watched it while doing nothing to stop it.

And as soon as things got complicated, I had the luxury of running away because I don't feel the way he does. That makes me a selfish coward. I should have just stabbed him in the heart. It might have hurt less than sleeping with him again.

I realize I've been staring at the little receipt at the pump a little too long. I tear it free, shove it into my purse, and make my way inside the convenience store. I hope caffeine and a snack will reset my brain.

That's when I see him.

No, not him him. Not Carter *him*. Jackson *him*.

He has a red Gatorade in his hand and his jaw is set in that kind of way where you just know the man is irritated. I happen to meet his eyes and give him a familiar smile out of habit.

"Hey," I offer.

He doesn't smile back, and sharply says, "Hey."

I tilt my head trying to read him. "Are you okay?"

"Yep. Fine," he snaps again, sounding even more irritated.

In between the chips and the Twix, I cross my arms in front of him. "What is your problem?"

He faces me, full-on stares me down like a disappointed father, and sneers. "My problem is that you're fucking with a guy who doesn't deserve it."

I feel like he's just splashed cold water on my face. "Excuse me?"

"You heard me. That shit you've been doing to Carter, screwing with a guy who would move the fucking moon and stars for you. That's my problem."

A woman sneaks in and steals a bag of pretzels from behind Jackson's frame. "Don't paint me out to be some manipulative villain. He knew exactly what this was from the start."

Jackson's stare doesn't waver. "Yeah. He did. But that doesn't make it okay."

"I didn't promise him anything."

"No," he says, stepping closer, "but you knew. You saw the shift. You watched him fall, and you kept showing up anyway."

"I didn't *let him* do anything," I snap. "He's an adult. He could've walked away anytime."

Jackson leaned in, voice sharp. "He's stupidly in love with you. It's kinda sick how you know it, and you still keep going back. You keep letting him believe that maybe this time you'll feel the same."

I look away. "It's not that simple."

"It is," he said, softer now. "You should've pulled back. Should've been honest. Not for you—for him. Calling him these past few weeks was a mistake. You knew you still didn't want more, but yet he came running to you every time because he loves you and wants you to see it."

I don't have a comeback that doesn't sound like a sorry excuse. Because everything he's saying? It's not wrong. He's read me and Carter's *thing* like an open book, and now I'm the antagonist in my own story.

"Look, whoever you really are, '*Venus*', you're not a bad person," he says, "But you're doing a bad thing. You're playing with my best friend's feelings like putty and I don't like it. You're just going to break him."

"I still don't understand how this is my fault." My voice cracks a little, more frustration than volume. "Why is it always the woman who gets blamed for feelings? Callie said the same thing to me. Apparently I signed up to be the bad guy in someone else's fantasy. I didn't ask for any of this."

"Maybe you didn't ask for it, but it happened, and you let it. That's why you're the bad guy. If you don't feel that way about him, that's fair, but at least break it off for his sake. He's in too deep and I don't think he has it in him to be the one to let this go. You have to do it."

"You don't get it," I mutter.

"Then explain it."

"You're acting like I don't care about him at all, like I want to hurt him. I like him. Is that what you want to hear? I *like* Carter, a lot. But he knows why I don't want commitment, and I'm not changing that because things got messy. I've been clear with him from the start."

"All of that would have been fine if you had let him go. But you didn't. You've called him every time you've gotten lonely and he came running like a lousy puppy to his owner. And now you're throwing a tantrum and acting like a selfish brat because *you* played with *his* feelings. You let him fall for you until he was in a hole he can't climb out of anymore." He takes a deep breath, and I'm stuck staring at him. He turns from me. "I said what I needed to say. Enjoy that commitment-less life. I hope the sex was worth breaking him."

And just like that, he walks off, checks out at the cashier, and leaves. When I get back into my car, I just...sit. No music. No tears. No A/C.

Just as I'm getting ready to leave, my phone buzzes with a new text.

Carter: Come over?

I stare at his name for a long time. I type the word *no* and hover my thumb over the send button.

Then I clear the text box and retype *yes*.

And just like that, I realize I really am the villain.

Chapter 22 | Vulcan

I don't know at what point I lost all my dignity, but like always, my only way to see her was a promise of sex, even if that's not really what I wanted from this. It's the only way she'll give me the time of day.

I'm still stupidly hoping that one day, I'll open the door, and she'll jump into my arms rom-com style and everything will be okay after that.

But it never is. It's our same routine. She gets here, I lick her pussy, we make a mess of each other, and she leaves. She leaves like it's so easy for her when it kills me each time she walks out of the door.

She didn't leave last night, though. She stayed over, slept in my arms, and then woke up with that *'this was a mistake'* look she gives me every time. I don't really know when this shift happened.

Everything was going so well and then one day, it wasn't. I don't even think it was the forehead kiss that did it, either. I think she realized she was falling too, even just a little bit, and it scared her.

Now, she acts like I'm a stranger again, and I don't know how much more of it I can take. How much more am I willing to put myself through for a girl who has told me time and time again that she doesn't want me?

She gives me the grace of letting us stop for coffee together before our shifts, but mine has been cold for a long time. I haven't touched it. It's not like it would make me feel any more alive.

We sit in a corner booth, awkward silence filling the space between us. The hiss of the espresso machine on the other side of the cafe does its best impression of white noise, but it does nothing to ease the tension. I have my boot propped up on the opposite bench, absently but maybe purposefully locking her in the booth so she can't run until we finally talk about this, because I can't move on until I know for sure where we stand.

The coffee shop is mostly empty and everyone inside is half-asleep. But not me. I'm fully awake and aware of the woman sitting across from me.

She scans the room like she's expecting to get ambushed, but it's just me and her. The second she accidentally meets my eyes, she shrinks into herself like a puppy getting scolded by her owner.

She takes a deep breath. "Will you just tell me what's going on with you today?"

I run my hands through my hair, jaw tight. I've been rehearsing this for a while, trying to remember everything I want to say, but suddenly, I can't remember any of it. I default to the only thing I can truly remember.

"I've fallen for you," I say, looking down as if how my heart feels about her is something I should be ashamed of. She straightens her spine—I can see it from the corner of my eye. I lift my head to examine her face, trying to find out what she's going to say before it falls from her lips.

The curve of her mouth turns slightly down. Her fingers toy with the sleeves of her hoodie. Her eyes are beautiful but distant. I think at this point, I could fall in love with her a hundred times over and still notice something new and beautiful about her.

She gives me a look like I've just spoken a foreign language.

I sigh. "I know, V. I know this wasn't the deal and you said no strings, but I can't pretend anymore. You deserve to know how I truly feel and I need to say it, at least once."

She doesn't flinch away or grow any more stiff than she already is, but she does lean back against the sticky seat of the booth and stares ahead at nothing.

"You already know what I'm going to say," she says, without meeting my eyes.

"Yeah. That you don't want this. You don't want me."

Her head turns to me. "Don't say it like that. Don't make it seem like I've hurt you. We made the decision to hookup when we wanted."

"We also made a promise to be honest with each other, and we both have been. When we started this, I had every intention of getting you to fall for me back, I did. But then you made it so clear that you didn't want that, so I followed your rules best I could. But...I can't do that anymore. I don't want to."

She looks at me, and her stare is brutal. Not because it's hateful or cold, but because it's...emotionless. "Okay. So what do you want to do about this?"

"The truth would be a nice start," I answer. "I know you didn't want serious a few months ago, but what about now? What about us? Doesn't it feel like more than just a hookup to you? Don't...don't I mean more than that to you?"

She doesn't answer. Just sighs.

Her silence is answer enough, so I add: "I'm not trying to get you to be someone you're not, but you can't ask for my body anymore and expect me to pretend I don't care about *you*."

She nods. "I know."

And for one second, one fucking second, I thought she might meet me halfway.

"So I think we shouldn't see each other anymore."

Her words knock the air right out of me. I stare at her like I didn't hear her right. Like maybe she said those words, but they came out wrong. She misspoke. I misunderstood.

Her voice goes quiet. "You're a good guy, Carter. I've told you what I can't give you and what we can't have together. You deserve a girl who can give you those things. Someone who wants the same things as you, without all this...complication."

My shoulders sag. "You're not even gonna try?" I ask, and my voice cracking gives away the hurt in my chest. "You're just...walking away from this?"

"Carter, there was never a 'this', there was never an 'us'. I told you from the beginning it wouldn't happen. I respect you for being honest with me, and I'm sorry I can't be that girl for you, but if you truly feel that way, then we don't need to drag this out. It wouldn't be fair to you."

"V, please," I beg, actually *beg*. "Don't give up on this yet. If you walk away I...I just don't want to look back on everything we've done together and the memories we've made and resent them. I don't want to look back and realize that none of it mattered to you."

She hesitates, and the silence between us turns from an uncomfortable tension to painful finality.

"It did matter. It did. But...it ends here." She reaches across the table like she didn't just rip my heart out and strokes her hand along my cheek. I lean in on instinct and she kisses me softly on the cheek.

Just enough to wreck me a little bit more.

"I'm sorry, Carter."

And then with that, she stands up and leaves, sliding out of the booth and walking out the door without looking back.

I don't stop her. Why would I?

I sit at the cafe for so long that I'm nearly late for my shift. When I get to the bunk room, I stare at the dusty ceiling with my arms crossed and my throat aching, trying to figure out how to let her go.

Not because I want to, but because I need to if I'm going to survive this heartbreak.

Chapter 23 | Venus

It's been two weeks since I've seen Carter. Two weeks of pretending our distance was mutual, that it was chosen by the two of us and isn't something I'm trying to hide behind.

We ended things clean, at least from my view. No dramatics, no screaming, no tears. We simply acknowledged it wasn't working for us, even though it was for entirely different reasons.

What we had was supposed to be fun, and it was never meant to be more than that. I can't necessarily blame him for catching feelings. If I'm being honest with myself, we really did get along and spending time together was thrilling and memorable. I suppose this was inevitable, but we still agreed not to take it too far.

I didn't want to steal his dignity by having that kind of conversation in public, and I didn't want him to get up and chase me. So I didn't leave the door open for him to follow. I simply ended things.

Two weeks later, I still tell myself it was the right call. I pat myself on the back for walking away when I did.

I still respect him for being honest with me even though it didn't work out for us in the end.

I fill the days with work, picking up extra shifts when I can to keep my mind occupied. We didn't technically break up, but it sort of feels that way when I catch myself scrolling through our old messages just to reread his bad jokes that made me laugh.

On a random Wednesday, I check my phone after missing a call from my dentist to see that he texted me hours ago and I didn't notice.

Carter. Just his name showing up on my screen makes my stomach flip.

Carter: Hey. We're going to be at Schooner's tonight. I thought I'd ask if you and some of your friends wanted to come.

Carter: I miss hanging out with you. We were good at that part.

I stare at my screen and I can practically feel him staring back, waiting for my little chat bubble to signal that I'm typing a reply. I hesitate for a long time before responding.

Me: Maybe. I'll ask them. We've had a busy week.

Carter: No pressure. Just let me know.

I consider for a while just waiting for an hour or two and then giving the overused excuse of being tired, and I even type it out on my keyboard, each letter chipping away at my heart.

I delete it as soon as I finish.

Me: Okay. We'll come. See you soon.

Schooner's is the same as it's always been. Same people. Same sticky floors. Same Christmas lights that haven't been taken down since 2004. Nothing's changed. The pool balls are still cracking against each other. The bar seats are peeling up vinyl. It smells like stale beer and cheap cologne.

It makes my heart squeeze, because this was ours once. Carter and I met here. Whatever we have—or had—it all started in this very bar. Before the tension and the silence and the awkwardness, this was ground zero. It was neutral territory before I started rebuilding walls I don't actually want to live behind, but too afraid to leave.

Callie is with me. She's the only one who was game for it. I don't think she came for the fun and the drinks though. I think she came for me. To watch over me. To look out for me. To stop me from making any more mistakes.

I find myself searching for him, feeling an ache in my ribs where he used to kiss me there.

I see him, in a corner all by himself. Hoodie, jeans, and boots as if he's trying to hide himself. He looks wrecked. Not like the Carter I knew before...*us*.

And this is exactly what Jackson was talking about when he said I broke him, but Carter doesn't have the strength to leave me behind.

The moment he sees me, he gives me that goddamn smile, doing a really good job at pretending he's okay. Like seeing me fixed his world instead of ruined it. I give him an Oscar-worthy smile back and slide into the booth across from him.

"Hey," he says, eyes crinkling in the corners.

"Hey," I say back. Too casual. Too calm. Too normal.

"I'm uh, honestly surprised you came tonight." He chuckles like he feels ridiculous. "Thought for sure you'd back out."

"I thought about it," I admit.

"What made you change your mind?"

I take a deep breath. "Maybe I just missed this part too," I say quietly, giving a nod to his earlier text. He gives me a smile, a real one, and just like that, the weirdness begins to crack and fade away.

There it is, the click. The shift. The gravity pulling us back into orbit around each other, like two planets fighting for their celestial love despite never getting close enough to touch.

I looked up the mythology around Venus and Vulcan. Right when Carter gave me the nickname and told me that they were close, I researched the ancient love story.

I found out that in Roman mythology, Venus is the villain in their love story, shredding away all the affection with Vulcan in their marriage until she took to finding other lovers. She's most famous for her infidelity, not her love.

It's a terrible story, really. I'm not sure Carter understood how fatal their attraction was when he gave me the nickname to match his.

From the corner of my eye, I see Callie and Jackson talking it up at the bar, both of them with their eyes set on me in anticipated disappointment. It's fair, but it's also not. I didn't come here with the intention of making things worse.

I think Carter feels it too. The way our small talk ends in awkward smiles. The way our laughter doesn't seem to come from a genuine place. How our sips are placed in between each topic like a lifeline. We're being careful, but it's just making it more painful.

Eventually, with a bad joke about Carter's terrible taste in beer, something between us shifts and the weirdness begins to crack. Little by little, we open up again until the smiles are real and the laughter comes from our chests.

Little by little, I forget to keep my guard up and he forgets about the distance he was trying to keep. Somewhere between the music and the fourth round of drinks, Carter ends up on my side of the booth.

Jackson, Trevor, and Callie shove themselves into the opposite booth, and I see a hopeful glimmer in Callie's eyes when she looks at Jackson. Like there's a spark there, and honestly, I hope there is.

Just because Carter and I didn't work out that way, doesn't mean something else can't come out of our new friend group.

As I finish that thought, Carter leans over. "You look good," he says, his voice low and a little bit slurred. The hum of the jukebox in the background playing a country ballad makes this moment feel more charged than it should be.

"So do you," I whisper back, my breath fanning across his ear.

His breath quivers on his next inhale, and I lean away, taking a long swig of my drink. The ballad continues playing and I make up some sorry excuse about how I hate the song even though I really don't. I slide out of the booth and Carter follows me to the jukebox. We stand shoulder-to-shoulder, flipping through all the familiar song titles without really caring what we choose.

It's just an excuse to be close, and we both know it.

He turns to me, a little buzzed and a little unsteady. But his eyes tell me everything he wants to say before it falls out of his uncoordinated lips.

"Let's get out of here," he says.

I nod. "Yeah. Okay."

We're a little too tipsy to drive, so we take a short cab ride to my place. It's quiet, the only noise in the car is the soft tunes the driver is playing. Carter's hand brushes my knee, and that's where it stays, his pinky rubbing back and forth on the fabric of my leggings.

When we get to my apartment, he changes, suddenly stiff and acting as though he's never been there, too afraid to even ask to sit down.

I set my bag on the counter and turn to him, and suddenly the both of us are very sober and wondering if it was a mistake all over again.

"You still know how this ends," I say, firmly. I don't want him to think of this as anything other than what it is—two friends hooking up.

He looks at me and his eyes are glossing over with a hundred things he wants to tell me. He lets out a big sigh, and finally says: "I know."

I don't answer. Instead, I close the distance between us and kiss him. Slow. Familiar. Safe. The kind of kiss that tells him that this isn't meaningless, even if it should be.

Our clothes disappear, one after the other until we're both naked in each other's arms and wrapped up together in my thin sheets.

He slides into me without any resistance, grinding his hips in a slow and steady pace. I wrap my legs tight around his hips, anchoring us together. His mouth doesn't leave mine, swallowing my soft moans as I tug on his hair and roll my hips to meet his.

The wet heat between our bodies begins to drip onto the sheets, but we don't stop. We're not even chasing release, we're just...connected.

Somehow that makes it all more devastating.

His hands find mine tangled in the sheets and he laces our fingers together above my head, trapping me in the intensity of the moment. I can't move, and I don't want to.

I just want him. That's it.

And I'll tell him in the morning.

But for now? I let him make love to me.

When we both grow tired and he finishes deep inside me, I lie with my head on his chest as he traces patterns up and down my back.

This silence doesn't scare me. Not tonight.

Chapter 24 | Vulcan

I'm sitting on the edge of her bed, shirt in my hand, elbows on my knees. My heart is doing that thing where it unevenly thumps when my brain finally catches up with my reason, waiting for me to admit the hard stuff out loud.

The silence between us is thick and foreboding, like a dense fog in a zombie movie. It's uninviting and creeping between us like a wedge.

Behind me, V wakes up, stretching and shifting against the pillows. The heat of us still lingers on the bedsheets, but somehow, nothing feels warm anymore.

"Carter?" I hear her say, her voice quiet and steady. "Are you...okay?"

I don't answer right away, and I don't have the strength to look at her either. My eyes stay glued to the floor, like I'm waiting for a script to write itself in the carpet.

I let out a breath. "We shouldn't have done this again."

She sits up, I can hear it in the rustle of the sheets and see the movement out of the corner of my eye. "What do you mean?"

I finally look at her, and it fucking hurts. She's right there. So close. Bare skin. Tangled hair. Lips I've memorized a hundred times over.

Yet she couldn't feel any further away if she tried.

"I thought...I thought I could handle this," I explain. "The casual, no strings thing. I thought I could just be the guy you called when you wanted company and I'd learn to be okay with it. I really did, V. But I can't do it."

"Carter—"

"I love you," I say, finally tearing off the bandage. "But I don't want to love you like this."

"Carter—"

"I know. I know this isn't what you want, but I had to say it. I had to tell you the truth. As much as I want you, I don't want to live in this lie anymore."

She shifts closer, reaching for me, but I stand from the bed and take a step away, putting space between us like I'm drawing a new line in the sand she's not allowed to cross.

"I'm not trying to shift the blame or make you feel bad," I continue. "I knew what this was and I can't hold you responsible for feelings that I developed on my own."

"Carter, listen—"

"I mean, I don't even know your name, right?" I chuckle humorlessly to myself. "I can't keep pretending I'm okay with this when I'm not."

"Carter!" she shouts to get my attention. "What are you trying to say?"

"That I don't want to keep acting like this doesn't matter to me. Like you, we, *us* doesn't matter to me. And I know I can't flip a switch and force you to fall in love with me back."

"It does matter to me, though," she pleads.

"Not in the way that's enough for me. I've showed up every time you asked, because I thought maybe if I gave you what you want for long enough, you'd see me as something more than a quick fuck. But you have your reasons, and you don't, and I'm tired of pretending that doesn't cut me open every time we say goodbye."

Something in her face shifts, and it looks like she might actually start crying. "But I thought you said you'd stay here if I started running?"

I scoff. "Yeah, I did. But you never started, did you?"

She gives me a guilty look. She understands exactly what I'm saying.

"I'm just telling you where I'm at. You don't want more, and I do. That's not changing."

She turns her face away. I nod, because even now, she won't say anything. Won't meet me halfway, won't even give me hope. My frustration is on full display now, and I finally pull my shirt back down over my head like armor. Then I grab my hoodie and wallet.

"Carter," she says softly, holding the sheets up to her chest as she stands and grabs my wrist. "I..." she gulps.

I pull my arm out of her soft grip. "You don't have to pretend anymore. It's okay. We had our fun, but it's over now."

"Wait!" she yelps. I pause. She stares. "I was going to tell you this morning. I...I changed my mind."

"Changed it about what? Us? About wanting more? Do you really want my dick that badly that you'd lie straight to my face as I'm walking out the door? Don't bullshit me, V."

I shake my head and turn. I don't even bother to look at her, and it breaks my heart that she doesn't even try to convince me that I'm wrong. That this isn't all some last-ditch effort to keep me as a bootycall.

That she really wants us to be something more.

But she doesn't. I knew she wouldn't.

So I walk out quietly, with the door clicking shut behind me. Punctuation to a final 'goodbye' neither of us had the strength to say.

I don't look back.

But fuck, do I want to.

Chapter 25 | Vulcan

The common room is holding it's breath, like it's waiting for something. We can all feel it. The silence, the tension. It's thick in the air like black smoke. The calm before a storm. We're all on edge and every sound has us jumping and ready for an alarm.

I sit on the edge of my cot, half-dressed and fully wrecked. Boots on, jacket open. My fingers grip the fabric of my pants like if I rip through them it'll let the pain in my chest fall out of the hole. V's voice is still stuck in my head.

She met my feelings with such hostility every time I tried to approach our situation with tenderness. I tried, I really did, to make it work her way, and I tried damn hard to get her to have a little faith in me.

In the end, all I got was a broken heart.

And her? I'm not sure I left any impression at all.

She never did anything that she didn't warn me about. That's the worst part. She's right—I knew what this was from the beginning. She got to walk away clean, and I'm still bleeding.

Maybe she shouldn't have kept calling me, but I also shouldn't have kept running back. We're both at fault for that, and it hurts.

Across the room, Trevor is eating Twizzlers like it's the solution to all the world's problems. If I wasn't on shift, I'd be halfway in the bottle. Trevor holds out the bag to me, beckoning me to take a rope.

"If you keep staring at the floor like it's gonna apologize to you, I'm gonna start worrying," he says, candy dangling from his mouth. "At least talk to me, bro. Let me in like a good boy."

I snort.

He shrugs. "It's fine. You don't have to say anything. Cooter's heart's a little sensitive right now."

Despite his annoying teasing, I'm glad he's here for me, even if he won't say it directly. After the pain and quiet Venus left behind, it's nice to know that his dumb commentary and stubborn loyalty are a constant in my life that I never have to worry about losing.

It might as well be the only thing keeping me upright.

My fingers just grip a piece of candy from his bag when the alarm hits. Both of us drop everything, and sprint to our gear.

Dispatch to Engine One. Structure fire in Mercer Street's Industrial District. Workers unaccounted for.

Captain Rodriguez answers the call on the radio, confirming that we're on our way with the engine and requests backup ambulances just in case.

We move fast. Faster than fast. This is the kind of call we've been anticipating all day.

And for some reason, I feel an anxious knot in my stomach, like this is the type of fire that will burn before I even see the flames.

The building is screaming by the time we get there.

It's a three-story warehouse with a brick shell, belching smoke out of every window and poisoning the air around it as easily as food coloring in water. We can feel the heat from the street. It's suspected to have started as an electrical fire, and I'm not surprised. These older buildings sometimes can't handle the new-age machinery and it overheats the breaker boxes. I've seen it a lot in this town, but usually the fires are handled with an extinguisher and a fast-acting worker.

This is probably the biggest structure fire I've ever seen in my time, and I have a feeling it will stick with me for a long time. But I love these fires, because they're learning opportunities. When we get back to the station, we can go over what we can do better, and I live for that just as much as I do the flames. I want to be Fire Chief someday, and these are the kinds of experiences I need to earn that honor.

"Westwood!" Rodriguez shouts. "We've got two unaccounted for. Take Knight with you. Search and rescue. Get in, get out, structure's compromised."

Trevor and I give each other a nod and don our masks. Jackson stops us. "Hey, be careful. Third floor's already partially collapsed." He points toward one of the large, busted out windows on the second floor where you can just see the flooring of floor three falling into floor two. He motions to Trevor. "Let me go instead. Stay with the engine."

"Yeah right," Trevor says, passing his Halligan from one hand to the other. There's no time to argue, so Trevor follows me in, leaving Jackson to operate as point on getting the fire under control and to keep it from spreading to other buildings in the District.

We enter the building on instinct. The heat hits us like a punch. We move fast, finding the first worker near a back wall, burned and barely conscious. We drag him out in less than a minute, hand him off to the medics, and don't even stop for a breath before we're back inside.

In the few seconds we were outside, things inside the building got much worse. Thicker smoke, hotter fire, flames shooting out in every direction like tendrils reaching for us.

Something in the air feels off. Wrong. Bad. Like the building doesn't want us there anymore, but there is still one civilian unaccounted for, and I'd die before I leave someone behind.

We clear the entire first floor and find nothing, so the both of us carefully make our way up the concrete staircase to the second floor. It's even hotter up here, and we both know we're running out of time. We do our best to crawl through the building, practically blind, when over the roar of the fire, we hear a crash and a scream.

"Back corner!" Trevor yells, shining his head light in the direction. There's a woman there, pinned under collapsed shelving. She's screaming desperately for help. Trevor and I have no time to sigh in relief as we unpin her and I hold her up under her shoulders to help her out. Trevor watches my back as we make our way back downstairs and out the building.

"Take her!" I shout at Jacks, waiting there with a group of paramedics nearby. He takes her from my arms. I turn to make sure Trevor's still behind me, but my heart stops.

He's gone.

Crack. I hear the building start to come down, but I go back into the flames to look for my friend. I don't think, I just run.

"Trevor!?"

Just at the staircase we came down, part of the building has collapsed. And there, half-buried under steel and blood soaking through his pant leg, is Trevor.

Chapter 26 | Vulcan

"Fuck," I spit under my breath.

The building is coming apart and we are seriously running out of time. The fire is screaming through the walls like a wild animal, the smoke clawing at my mask like it's ready to suffocate me. The fire surrounds me like it's ready to feed on my flesh.

But I keep moving deeper into the flames, toward Trevor. I yell his name over the roar, and I feel my heart sink when I don't hear him respond.

"Trevor!"

Another silent step. Then another. Then another.

And then—

"Carter!" I hear through a choked cough.

He's fully pinned under a support beam, thick, splintered, and scorched by the heat. I'm not even sure he feels the pain in his leg where a stick of rebar has gone clean through, because his jacket is torn at the shoulder and the skin underneath is black and burnt to the bone.

"I can't move," he says frantically. Scared. No—terrified. "It's crushing my leg. You have to go. Now—"

"Shut the fuck up," I growl, trying my best to lift the heavy beam. "You go, we go."

"Fuck those sentiments, Carter. This is real life. You stay, we both die."

"Then I'm dying with you," I yell back. My gloves hit the floor as I reach for his discarded Halligan and go straight for the beam, rage in my jaw and panic bubbling high in my chest. It doesn't move. I growl through my teeth. "Come on!" I scream as I try again, putting everything I have into it.

The beam shifts. Just an inch.

Trevor screams, and the sound cuts straight through me like a razor.

The roar of the smoke changes and we both look up. It's thicker now. Darker. Hotter.

We both know what that means.

Flashover is coming, and we have seconds.

I look back towards the exit, and a very cowardly part of me weighs if I can make it in time. Instead, I pull out my radio.

"*Mayday, mayday, mayday*. Engine One interior. We are trapped. I repeat, we are trapped."

I drop the radio, not really caring if anyone responds at all, as I go back to trying to lift the beam. I hear a snap and then a rush of heat at my back.

Then something hits me, hard. A falling beam, or maybe the entire second floor. I just know my mask is now pressed against the concrete and the wind is knocked out of my lungs from the impact.

My mask has a crack in it. My hip feels dislocated. I can't breathe anymore. My mask begins to fog up and I'm practically blind.

I try to move, but I can't.

"Carter!" Trevor yells, reaching for me. I reach back, and we take each other's hands as our PASS devices start blaring an alarm, signaling to everyone else how absolutely fucked we are. "I told you to get out!"

The heat is impossible now, like being tossed into Hell itself.

I squeeze his hand even tighter, and I think we both realize at the same time that this really is it.

"I love you, brother," I tell him. Not loud, not frantic. Just the truth. Something calm and steady in our last moments.

He nods, eyes wet, body trembling from adrenaline and pain. "Yeah, love you too."

The air shifts, and everything around us stills for a brief second before the roar of the fire consumes us in flashover. The whole room bursts into impossibly hot flame.

I hear the both of us screaming through the agony and the terror, but I never let go of his hand, and he never lets go of mine.

Then, silence.

Heat gone.

Light gone.

Just...nothing.

Chapter 27 | Venus

I'm in the middle of a delivery when Callie sneaks into the room. I give her a smile, but she doesn't even seem to register that I'm there. Instead, she goes straight for the attending and whispers in her ear. After a short conversation, my charge nurse approaches me and quietly says I need to head to the nurse's station immediately for an emergency.

I give her a strange look. As if the baby currently crowning mid-push isn't enough of an emergent situation. My hands freeze, just for a second, but then I do as I'm told. I peel my gloves off, toss them in the trash can, and give my hands and arms a good scrub before stepping out of the delivery room.

I walk to the station with half-haste and half-hesitation. I turn the corner, and everything just...stops.

Jackson is standing there in full gear, covered in soot. Helmet off, eyes red-rimmed and filled with pain. The kind of expression that you only give when there's news no one wants to say out loud.

I rush to him. "Carter? Oh God, is he okay?"

He doesn't answer. He grabs my wrist and firmly pulls me along with him. My heart is beating out of my ribs as I practically have to jog to keep his pace. "Jackson, please, what happened?"

He doesn't look at me. "You need to see it for yourself."

He brings me straight to the ER, where the lights are too bright and the smell is too sterile. But there's a new smell now, something that makes your stomach curdle. Burnt flesh.

We stop in front of a triage room, and I feel like I can no longer breathe.

Carter is laid out on the trauma bed like a lifeless doll. Tubes are down his throat. IVs are in both of his arms. Half of his face is burned, and his clothing is stuck to his cooked flesh in chunks. The rest of him looks inhuman. his arms are blistered and raw.

The kind of damage you don't come back from unscathed.

If. If you come back from it.

The world tilts and I catch myself on the wall of the hallway as an ER nurse bumps into me, rushing into the room with more supplies. My hands cover my mouth as I try to hold back the vomit in my throat.

It's like I can't breathe. The air is wrong. People are moving around him in an ugly, tragic dance of life-and-death.

"What happened?" I choke out.

Jackson's next to me, staring at his friend. "Warehouse fire. He was in there with Trevor looking for two missing civilians when the building came down on both of them. We heard his mayday but...but it was too late. The smoke hit the flashover point and there was nothing we could do to get them out."

"Where's Trevor?"

Jackson paused. His silence was more than answer enough. He shakes his head. The world stops moving, and my stomach sinks to the floor.

"Carter held on long enough for us to get him out but he crashed in the ambulance on the way here and..." his voice breaks and we can't finish his sentence.

I stare at the man in the trauma bed that I swore I couldn't fall in love with. The man I pushed away over and over because I was afraid of caring too much.

"He's stupid in love with you," Jackson says, and it's what forces the tears to fall from my eyes. "He'd want you here if he—"

Another voice crack. He doesn't have to say it.

I shouldn't but I push my way into the room and swoop under the bodies rushing past to grab Carter's wrist. One of the only places left that wasn't burnt raw. The only place safe to touch him. I close my eyes, block out the world and feel for his pulse.

And that's where I stay.

"I'm here," I whisper. "I'm not going anywhere."

I stand by his side for hours, until the triage is complete and they move him to the burn unit for observation. Jackson and I are there the entire time. Some of his team comes to visit, but Jackson and I are the only two that stay day and night.

Carter is burned. Badly. Second-degree burns over a third of his body, and third degree in big, thick patches across his back. His stability is shaky at best. Every alarm going off fills me with dread, like it will be the last one. He pulls through every time, but it doesn't do anything to settle my uneasiness.

In the middle of the night, Jackson finally dozes off, giving me a completely quiet moment in the chaos. I rest my forehead on that little patch of unburnt skin on his wrist, the only place I can safely touch.

"I'm sorry," I whisper to his still, gauze-covered body. "God, I'm so sorry. I'm sorry I didn't say anything sooner, but please don't die on me Carter. Let me have the chance to love you, okay? *Please.* I was so stupid for thinking I needed control. That I had to suppress my feelings, even after you told me you'd stay. And when I finally realized what I had right in front of me...it might have already been too late."

In the morning, I stand in the corner with Jackson while the workers on shift in the burn unit take care as they change Carter's gauze. They unwrap him like a mummy, and that sickness creeps back up my throat as I'm forced to look at his blistered, broken body.

Callie, bless her, arrives mid-day with a change of clothes for me and a turkey sandwich from my favorite sub shop just to keep me going.

The room is filled with get-well-soon cards, flowers, and balloons from the entire community. One card in particular got me.

It's from the young son of one of the workers he and Trevor saved that day. Words like 'hero' and 'awesome' fill the card, and at the end, the boy writes about how he wants to be a firefighter too, so he can save someone's dad just like Carter did.

I set the card to the side and hold my face in my hands as I cry, thinking about how if Carter doesn't make it, he's going to die thinking he was unloved because I was too afraid of my own feelings.

I wipe my face and go back to holding his wrist like I could transfer some of my life into him.

"Don't leave forever when I finally figured out how badly I want you to stay."

The next time the burn team comes in, the doctors talk about nerve ending and skin grafts, therapy for the dysmorphia that comes with burn injuries to the face.

Trevor's parents come to visit. His mom, who looks like a saint if I've ever seen one, collapses to her knees and prays for Carter, telling his sleeping body how proud she is of him and how happy he's alive, thanking him for trying to save her son. They must be close, because she fusses over him like a mother would, demanding answers about his condition and prognosis.

It warms my heart to see how much people in his life care for him. But none of that matters if he dies, does it?

Well into the night, when the rest of the world is asleep, I'm stroking Carter's wrist when I swear I feel a muscle twitch. My head jerks up, and I'm suddenly fully awake. I throw my empty coffee cup at Jackson's head to wake him up too.

"What!?"

I nod down. "Look!"

We both observe Carter's wrist for what feels like a solid hour, but he doesn't move again.

"I swear...I felt..."

And then his fingers twitch. Two of them.

I let out a sound of pure relief and lean over him, carefully cradling his head without touching him.

"Carter! Carter, it's me. It's Venus. It's okay. You're okay."

From under his bandages, his swollen eyelids flutter open, and I can't help the tears streaming down my face. Jackson's crying too.

"You're in the hospital," Jackson says. "You ever scare us like that again, I'm kicking your ass."

Carter starts fighting against an invisible force, probably unbearable pain, so I hit the nurse call button and gently stroke his wrist some more.

"Carter," I whisper. His eyes drift to me.

"Victoria. My name is Victoria."

He tries to say something, but all that comes out is a hoarse breath. I shake my head and place the most featherlight and careful of kisses to his bandaged nose.

"My name is Victoria, and I love you too, Carter Westwood."

Chapter 28 | Vulcan

Pain is all I know how to feel anymore. It's the first thing I felt when I woke up, and no amount of morphine makes it go away. A slow, aching throb wraps around my chest, threads through my ribs, and sinks deep into the bone marrow of my limbs. I can't move without pain. I can't blink without pain. I can't breathe without pain.

My name is Victoria, and I love you too, Carter Westwood.

I thought I had imagined her saying those words at first. Pain-induced delirium or some shit, but it was real. She was real. And she hasn't left my side once.

And Jackson is there too, giving me shit about almost dying and scaring him. He's still in his turnout pants, still streaked in ash and soot like he hasn't moved in days. He looks wrecked. Red around the eyes, every muscle stretched tight with worry and grief.

The weight of everything comes rushing back to me. Heavy and uncomfortably familiar. I give Jackson a look, and he gives me one right back.

My voice is a thin whisper. "Trevor?" I croak out.

Silence.

Jacks says nothing. His eyes drop, and I feel that dread in my chest before he opens his mouth.

"Jacks," I croak again. "Where is Trevor?"

His jaw clenched, and his eyes meet mine, even redder than before and brimming with tears.

"He didn't make it."

I don't feel the bed underneath me anymore, just an elephant in my chest, a knot in my stomach, and the sharp slice of unimaginable grief stabbing my chest.

I shake my head the best I can, making my skin burn even worse than it already is. "No," I say. Not a question. Not a plea. Just pure disbelief. "He...he...he was with me. The flashover hit and if I made it then so did he. Right? Right? You're...you're...you're fucking with me. You're—"

Alarms start ringing and my chest gives out. I can't breathe anymore. I crack open. A sound from another world escapes me, raw and guttural. My heartbeat monitor goes wild in protest. I begin to try and break free from my place on the bed, causing pain to blossom all over my body, but I don't care. I don't care about the burns or the wires or the machines. I don't even care about Jackson or Victoria.

Trevor is gone.

Trevor is gone.

Jackson and Victoria hold me down as gently as they can, trying to tether me to reality when all I want to do is go into the past and try harder to save my friend.

Maybe even die with him.

I give Jackson a pleading look. "Please, Jacks, this is a sick joke. Tell me you're lying to me."

His face twists in pain, and that's when I know he's telling the truth. My best friend is gone. My brother is gone.

I close my eyes, and the tears don't stop coming. The nurses administer more morphine and a mild sedative, but it does nothing to ease the ache in my chest.

I stare at the ceiling and cut everything and everyone out. I say nothing to no one. Not even the doctors or nurses coming to check on me. I just give them....nothing.

I'm still here, and he's not, because I didn't try hard enough to get him out.

Victoria holds my wrist tightly, grounding me, and I think it's the only thing keeping me from losing it completely.

Chapter 29 | Venus

He doesn't answer the door right away. I knew he wouldn't. He never does anymore.

I stand at his door, fingers tightening around the straps of my bag, forehead nearly pressed to the wood. The hallway is quiet, too quiet for a guy who used to blast classic rock from the kitchen while making me boxed mac and cheese in a pot way too big for the amount of food we need.

"Carter?" I call gently.

Nothing for a second.

Then the lock turns.

He opens the door, eyes bloodshot, face hollow. He looks like a shadow of the man I know—baggy sweats, a blanket falling off one leg, shirt rumpled like he hasn't bothered to change in days, or maybe even a full week. He doesn't speak. Just steps aside.

I try my best not to let my eyes linger too long on the burns. All things considered, he still looks like the Carter I fell in love with, but I can't imagine the psychological torture he's going through, looking in the mirror and seeing a permanent reminder of the worst day of his life.

He's scheduled for his official skin graft consultation after the funeral.

Carter refused to sit in the hospital any longer, leaving against medical advice, and forcing the doctors to plead with him to be careful. I promised I'd look after him, take care of his wounds, but burns aren't my specialty.

He doesn't let me in anymore, and the flames left just as much damage on his heart than his skin. I don't know how to *help* him.

"I brought soup," I say quietly, holding up the container like it was something that could bring him comfort. "And gauze. You haven't changed the dressing, have you?"

Still nothing.

I set the container down on the counter. His apartment smells like smoke and leftover antiseptic, and I hate how normal that feels now.

"You're supposed to be taking care of yourself," I say.

"I'm trying." He rubs his face, hissing when he touches the sensitive patches on his cheeks. "I just don't know what I'm doing."

I nod, already reaching into my bag. "Lift your shirt."

He obeys, slow and stiff. I peel back the old dressing. The wound looks angry. Red. Swollen. Healing slowly. His skin is hot under my fingers. I clean it gently, with careful hands, but I don't talk. He doesn't need words right now. He needs care. Small, quiet, deliberate support from someone that isn't from his fire station, mourning the same loss.

"I can't stop thinking about that day," he says suddenly, voice frayed.

I move to lean around him and meet his eyes, waiting for him to continue.

"One minute we were sharing candy. Then there was fire. Then he was gone." His throat moved like it hurt to speak. "I was holding his hand. It was all I could do, because I wasn't strong enough to get him out. I should have called the mayday sooner. I should have-"

"Carter," I say, quiet but firm, fingers stalling on his skin. I reach up, touched his jaw on a patch of skin that isn't burned and rub my finger back and forth before forcing him to look at me. "You did more than anyone else would have. And he knew that. We all do."

He breaks.

He folds into my arms like he can't be bothered to support his own weight anymore—like the world is too heavy on his shoulders. He tightly clutches my arms as I carefully wrap them around him, trying not to cause him pain. He sobs into the air, and I just hold him as he lets out raw, broken gasps of grief.

Minutes pass before he grows quiet. Then, he sits up, turns, and kisses me. It comes out of nowhere. It's not gentle or romantic. It's...wrecked. Desperate. Not in a lustful way, but like he's searching for a way to feel anything other than this pain he's working through. I let him do what he wants. He squeezes my breast under my hoodie, and kisses me again, harder now.

But then he breaks down again, because whatever he was searching for, he didn't find. He collapses into me again, wrapping his arms around me as tight as his injuries will let him. I stroke his hair and let him cry it out again, kissing the crown of his head and rocking him softly from side to side.

"I'm here," I whisper. "I know I ran before, but I promise I'm not going anywhere. I'm sorry it took nearly losing you to admit that, but whatever journey you have ahead of you, I'll be right by your side."

He sniffles into my chest, then whispers, "Just stay with me."

I nod against the top of his head. "Yeah. I'll stay."

And I do.

Chapter 30 | Vulcan

The sky looks like it hasn't seen the sun in days. It just hangs there—low and gray and heavy, tasting like rain that's waiting for a dramatic moment to fall. Dark, rumbling clouds stretch across the crowded cemetery.

The whole town has pressed pause on the day. People of all ages gathered to pay their respects to a man they don't really know.

My collar feels too tight, like it's intentionally suffocating me as I stand like a statue. One hand is clenched tightly at my side while the other is white-knuckling an umbrella. I can't feel my fingers. I can't feel my toes.

I can't *feel*.

The casket is too close.

It's not close at all.

But it's *too close*.

It's polished navy-blue. His favorite color. The flag that flew on the truck the day we lost him is lifted from his closed-casket and sharply folded into a triangle. Captain Rodriguez hands it's perfect corners to his sobbing mother like the precision could make up for everything the fire took from her.

Trevor would have hated this. The ceremony, the pageantry, the solemn quiet that no one is brave enough to break through. He would have made a joke about how the flowers look like dicks or how stiff we all look in our suits. I can almost hear him, like he's standing right next to me, watching us say goodbye to his unrecognizable body.

He would have laughed at me for being a sentimental bastard and shedding a tear when I was allowed to give his last call on the county radio station.

Attention all units. Attention all units.

This is Terracotta Fire Department Engine One Lieutenant Carter Westwood.

Driver Engineer Trevor Knight has answered his final call after six years of dedicated service to the Terracotta, Georgia community.

Be at peace now brother, we'll take it from here.

A long pause.

You go, we go.

Engine One, clear.

Victoria slides her hand into mine, loosening my fingers around themselves. She didn't ask or say anything. Just holds my hand.

I don't react at first. I can't. My eyes are stuck on that stupid wood box with my friend inside. Maybe if I stare at it long enough, he'll show up behind me, smack me on the ass and say: *"Awwww, did Cooter miss me?"*

But he won't. He can't.

The chaplain's voice fades in and out like static. Everyone's crying. Everyone's hugging.

But not me. I'm just staring at that box.

Trevor's mom is the first to approach me. She's clutching the folded flag tightly to her chest in her small, fragile, shaking hands.

I might as well be a second son to her, and she holds me like it. As soon as my forehead lands on her shoulder, I lose it. Ugly, gross, snotty sobs escape me and I think at this point I'm crying harder than she is.

"Oh, honey," she whispers, "I know you did everything you could. You were brothers. He wouldn't want you to cry for him."

I hear her words, but they don't register. I want to tell her that I'm sorry. I'm sorry I wasn't enough. I'm sorry I couldn't save him. I'm sorry I can't go back and switch places with him.

But I can't, so I just let her hold me while Victoria holds my hand. I crack wide open in front of all of them, and let them see everything I don't have the strength to say.

When his mom finally lets me go, his dad comes next. Then his sister. Then Captain Rodriguez. Then the community handing out thank-yous I don't deserve like Halloween candy.

Somewhere in the chaos of grief, I lose my grip on my sanity and walk away from the crowd, hiding behind the mausoleum away from all the eyes and the hugs.

Victoria comes around the corner, rubbing my shoulder with her steady hand.

I wipe my nose with my suit sleeve. "I just need a minute."

She nods. "I know. It's okay."

She lingers close by, close enough for strength, but far enough for space. The only person she lets get closer to me is Jackson, and when I meet his gaze, all those horrible feelings come back to me.

"Why him?" I ask Jacks, as if he could really give me an answer.

"You barely made it out yourself," Jackson says to me. Steady, but broken like the rest of us. "He wouldn't want you to blame yourself."

"He was always at my back. If I had just let him lead..."

"Then you'd be the one in the casket and he'd be here asking the same question. Carter, man, you were just doing your job. He trusted your judgement and he still would."

I lean my back against a tree and look to my right. V is watching us, but I can see it in her eyes that it's not right. Jacks and I are missing a very important part of ourselves.

We all walk back together, joining just in time for the salute. Three sharp cracks fill the air, and I don't even have the strength to flinch at the sound.

The ride home is silent. V doesn't force me to say anything. She just holds my hand while she drives.

When we get to my apartment, I panic, ripping and clawing in an attempt to get my crisp uniform off like it's poisoning my skin. V calms me down enough to help, undressing me like a toddler and sitting me down on the couch.

She squats in front of me and my blank stare, pushing my messy hair away from my red face.

"Talk to me," she says in a soft tone.

I shake my head. "I can't."

"You don't have to try and hold it in anymore. Not for me."

I open my mouth. Close it again. Open it again. Close it again.

Then it all spills out.

"I keep seeing it." My voice cracks. "The smoke. The beam. His face. The way he reached for me and the moment he realized I wasn't strong enough to get him out."

"You did everything you could, Carter."

"Yeah, everyone keeps saying that, but why does it feel like I didn't?"

She stands up then, and hugs my head into her stomach, stroking my hair while I breathe in the comfort of her scent mixed with rain. "Because grief doesn't operate on logic. It just...wrecks you. Unexpectedly. Unfairly. But it doesn't mean you didn't try your best. There's not a damn soul in this town that believes you would have left him behind. You almost died because you *refused* to leave him. And before you ask, I can't answer why you lived and he didn't, but I do know that the Carter Westwood I love would never leave his brothers behind."

'The Carter Westwood I love.'

Yeah, that breaks me. Completely. And she holds me through all of it.

"I don't know how to live in a world where he's not in it," I whisper into her stomach.

"One step at a time," she whispers. "One breath at a time."

She's not fixing it. She's not even trying to. She's just...here. Solid. Quiet.

Mine.

I pull back just enough to look up at her, and I know in this moment, that if I didn't have her, I'd be beyond saving right now.

"I'm a mess, V."

"So am I," she says. "But we'll just have to learn to clean each other up together. Deal?"

I nod. "Deal."

She leans down and kisses me on the forehead. Not because either of us expect it to fix anything or make me feel better right now, but because it reminds us both that no matter what comes next, we have each other.

Outside, the sky finally clears, letting a bright beam of sunlight light up the town.

The world and life moves on.

And I will too.

One breath at a time.

Epilogue | Vulcan

The shelter smells like wet dog, bleach, and pet food. Like hope and heartbreak all in one.

Dogs are barking from every direction. Some are bouncing off the walls from the sight of visitors. Others are tucked tightly into the corners of their little cages, their big wet eyes screaming terror. Some are cautiously approaching the steel doors to see what the commotion is about, defeated but hopeful.

I've got one arm thrown casually over Victoria's shoulder, both of us stopped in our tracks, staring through the bars of a kennel marked with a bright orange laminated sign:

Bonded Pair. Must Be Adopted Together. Bad With Children.

Inside, two pit bulls sit curled up like two halves of the same heart. Like if one moves, the other will move with them.

The bigger of the two, a male, tan in color, looks back at us with wide eyes and a heavy thump of the tail. His tongue lolls out like he's waiting to be called a 'good boy'. The other, a smaller, steel-grey female stays cautiously pressed against her brother, tail tucked in tightly next to her chunky body.

"They've been here a while," the animal shelter worker says. "It's hard enough finding someone willing to adopt one pit, but two? They're the sweetest babies in this shelter, though, and very loyal."

"They're perfect," I say. I look down at V, who has loosened herself from my grip and is squatting by the cage, beckoning the larger one over. He happily wags his tail but positions himself protectively between her and his sister. He pokes his nose through the bars and gives Victoria a sniff and a lick before going wild in the cage, jumping and wagging and barking. His excitement causes his sister to raise her head, and ever so cautiously, she gets closer and closer. At her own pace, she carefully sniffs the both of us, and then she sits.

Just sits. No indication of any excitement, but it's a very small sign of trust, and we couldn't ask for anything more.

V has a soft look in her eyes, tears filling her vision as she stares at the two pits, and her smile tells me everything I need to know.

"We'll take them," I say to the worker, and the best sound I hear all day is the little bell she rings at the front desk, twice, to show that two dogs have found a new forever home.

Our house isn't much, but it's ours. A little two-bedroom home, built in the early 1900's, with creaky floors and misaligned closet doors. The backyard is huge, and the neighbors are quiet. We're still in Terracotta, but on the outskirts where we have distance from the bustle of a busy small town, but still close enough to see the people we love.

The first few days with our new dogs are like heaven on earth. The male, who we named Nacho Cheese, took to the place like he owned it. He loves to be all over us, constantly. Every time you move, he moves, his tail wagging like a jet engine.

The girl though, named Cool Ranch, was a lot more wary of the house and her new family. She kept to herself mostly, enjoying her alone time in her little purple bed.

But one day, she decided that Victoria was safe, and now she sticks to her like glue. She loves me fine, and gives me plenty of kisses and snuggles, but I'm definitely the spare human in this case. My girls stick together, and that's more than okay with me.

The sounds of their claws on the hardwood is as normal as breathing.

So is their snoring.

Our home is full and beautiful, complete with the four of us. I've never been happier.

It's been a year since I lost Trevor.

A year since I lost my best friend. A year since I watched him disappear under smoke and steel. A year since I tried to save him, and failed.

I made it out. He didn't. And that's still impossible to accept to this day.

Therapy helped. A lot. Not right away, though. Not magically, and certainly not without some resistance from me.

But little by little, I got used to letting myself be vulnerable in my grief. In my guilt. In my fear. In the way that grief hollowed me out and left me just a little bit more rigid and sharp than I was before.

Some days I didn't say enough. Some days I said too much. Sometimes I didn't speak at all.

Victoria kept gently pushing me to stay consistent with my appointments, but she never asked for information I wasn't willing to share. She was there for me, but in a way that gave me quiet strength. A crutch to lean on while I learned to live with this hole in my chest again.

I still think of Trevor, and it still hurts. A photo of him, Jackson and I at our fire academy graduation sits on the table where we dump our house keys. His arms are slung over our shoulders, and we're grinning like idiots ready to face anything the world is willing to throw at us.

I see that photo every time I leave and every time I come home. I don't know if I could handle that if I didn't also come home to *her*.

My Venus. My Victoria.

She's never once run. Not even when I was at my worst. She kept showing up in my bed. And eventually, without even realizing it, her clothes were there. Her toothbrush was there. Her dirty scrubs landed in my washing machine, and I kept finding long blonde strands wrapped around my nuts.

That's when I knew it was forever.

One night in late spring, we've got citronella candles burning while we sit out on the back porch while Nacho Cheese chases brave rabbits through the backyard and Cool Ranch is curled up by our feet.

"Hey, V?" I say while I absently stroke her shoulder, barely pulling her attention from her mystery novel. She hums for me to continue. "I used to think life had a checklist. Marriage, kids, you know, the perfect little American Dream every country boy is expected to have."

Victoria eyes me suspiciously over the top of her novel. "And now?"

"Now I think life isn't something you can just...have. It's all of these tiny little choices we make that seem inconsequential at the time, but when you put them together, they give us...well, *us*. And losing Trevor really put into perspective just how...scary and unexpected things can get. I realized that chasing happiness in the future makes you miss out on everything you have *now*. I learned that all I want, I already have. You. The dogs. A good career."

She sets her book down and holds my hands. "I know what you mean about the unexpected. When

Jackson led me to the ER and I saw you that day...all I could think about was if you died, how much I would have regretted not loving you more. I never wanted to waste another minute with you, pretending my feelings weren't there. Sometimes I still get scared of the future, but our now is worth it."

I grin and say in a sing-songy voice: "Right here right now."

"Oh God," V playfully gags. "Did you really just reference High School Musical? Divorce. I'm taking the dogs."

"What's really worse? The fact that I referenced it, or the fact that you immediately recognized it?"

She glares at me, picks an ice cube out of her sweet tea, and shoves it down the back of my shirt. I laugh and grab one of my own, dropping it down the neck of her own shirt and getting it stuck in her bra.

We run into the yard and start chasing each other with ice cubes, our pits trailing behind to clean up the mess. Fireflies light up the air around us and the sun dips behind the horizon. The porch light flicks on automatically in the darkness.

V runs at me with her last ice cube and I catch her in my arms, spinning her in a circle in a fireman's carry until she's dizzy and begging me to stop. I set her on her feet and hold her.

Then I look at her. Really look at her.

This life isn't what I thought I wanted. It's better. Not because it was easy getting here, but because it's real. It's ours. It's messy and earned.

And I'll take this over any fairytale ending.

Or in our case, a mythological one.

Acknowledgements

This book is basically one big reference to my husband. So many of his quirks are woven into this story, and it made writing this so much more fun.

A huge shoutout goes out to his fire academy class, because the camaraderie demonstrated in this book directly parallels all the stories my husband shared with me while he was there.

Basically, what I'm trying to say is: *Mr. A, this one's for you.* Thank you for being my husband, my rock, my proofreader, and my insight into the male brain. I love you more than anything.

To my mother for your unconditional love, and to my dad, sitting in the afterlife with a beer in hand saying: *'I'm proud of you baby girl'.*

To my assistant, Samantha, who keeps me sane as I navigate this crazy little life and business.

To my cats, Burnt Toast and Lemon Pepper, who were nothing but nuisances like their mommy.

I always thank my readers, but this time, I want to highlight each and every one of you a little more. My life has completely changed for the better because of you giving my books a chance. It hasn't always been easy, but it has always been worth it. You've all brought joy into my life that I didn't know I could have. I'm so afraid that one day I will wake up and this will all be a dream, so I bask in the light you all bring to me every day.

Made in the USA
Monee, IL
29 August 2025

23358335R00115